ONE WEEKEND IN MONTANA

CADENCE KEYS

1

MAGGIE

My truck bumped over the slight divots in the uneven back road I took on my way to the bar on Main Street. I loved driving this way, country music blaring and blue skies ahead. But my favorite reason for taking this out-of-the-way route was so I could see the large farmhouse that I'd been stupidly in love with my entire life.

I rounded the slight bend in the road and my heart plummeted as I saw the bright red "Sold" sticker over the "For Sale" sign that had been sitting in front of the farm-house for the last several months.

My nose prickled, but I forced the emotions down with a sniff and a stiff upper lip. This wasn't my first go-round with disappointment, and knowing my luck, it wouldn't be my last. It was a pipe dream anyway. Even if the house had been on the market for another year, I probably wouldn't have been able to save up enough to buy it, especially considering all the other expenses in my life I could barely afford.

I had too many dreams and not enough money to make any of them happen.

I ignored the disappointment sitting heavy in my chest as I pulled up behind the old brick building that housed the reason I was stuck in Meadowbrook and couldn't afford to buy my dream house. Duke's Bar was a staple in downtown and had been in my family for most of my life. My dad opened it when I was five, and I'd grown up in that bar. It was exactly how you'd imagine an old, dingy bar in small-town Montana. The red brick was chipped in some places and cracked in others. The simple bar logo was painted on the window now since the design that had been branded above the door was so faded. Every six months or so, I'd have to touch up the paint, although what I really wanted to do was change it completely.

I walked through the back door and down the narrow hallway with the bathrooms on one side and the combination storeroom and office on the other. The hallway opened up to a dark space with the bar on the right with old wooden stools for patrons. Across from the bar were secondhand wooden tables that were older than I was and showed every sign of their age. The yellow lights that hung above them were outdated and permanently dusty, no matter how frequently I tried to clean them. A pool table with worn green felt was on the left side of the bar.

My body sagged with the desire to modernize this place. Lighten it up a bit—make it feel brighter and more inviting. Maybe even add to the menu to drive more sales, but things like that took money and time—neither of which I was flush with.

I quickly ran through my usual routine to get the bar ready and then at one o'clock on the dot, I unlocked the door and flipped the switch to light up the neon open sign that hung in the window. My dad had installed it six years ago—before his accident, which had put all my plans for the future on hold so I could stay in Meadowbrook to take care of him and run the bar. My brother had already been in college at Clark Fork University about an hour away and had a great job with a company in Missoula with a lot of growth potential—the kind of potential that had him moving to Portland, Oregon for his dream job after he graduated. I wasn't about to ruin his dreams when he was so close to achieving everything he'd worked so hard for.

My brother and my dad were the only people in the world I loved—besides the one man I refused to think about or acknowledge. My purpose in life had shifted to focus on them, and most of the time I was okay with that. It was only those quiet moments at night when my chest ached something fierce that I wished I'd get to do something for me for once. That one of my dreams could come true.

But as I had been reminded on my way into town when I'd seen that "Sold" sign, all my dreams seemed completely out of my reach.

Owning that old farmhouse was another thing I could cross off the list of dreams that had gotten shorter and shorter with every year.

In fact, the older I got, the more I realized it was stupid to have much hope at all. If I'd learn to stop hoping for things, then I wouldn't be so disappointed when they didn't happen.

The bell over the door chimed as my first patron of the day entered. "Heya Maggie."

"Hey Marcus, how was the fishing this morning?"

He waved his hand in the air before sitting at my bar where I had a coaster and his favorite beer already waiting. "No bites today."

"Bummer."

"There's always tomorrow," he said before taking a sip of his beer. It was what he said anytime he had a bad fishing morning.

Right on time, Lyle walked in and took a seat next to Marcus. "My usual, please, Maggie," he said before turning to Marcus. They talked about their customary round of topics—the fish, the *Yellowstone* wannabes that were ruining our state, and any other random topic that came to mind.

A few other regulars trickled in around the same time they did every day, sitting in their regular spots and ordering their usual drinks. Apart from my best friends, Sav and Joni, these were some of my favorite people in town. They'd known me since I was tiny, but they still respected me as the owner of this establishment. It might've taken a few years for them to get used to me running things instead of my dad, but we'd found our happy ground.

While I was getting a drink for Sal, another regular,

the door opened and I glanced back to see who it was, but the brightness outside put the large body in shadow as the man walked in. I focused back on the beer I was pulling so I wouldn't overfill it and heard the newcomer walk up to the bar. Without looking at him, I grabbed a cardboard coaster and set it down on the bar top and then handed Sal his beer.

I settled my hands on my hips, finally facing the newcomer, but the words I was about to ask died on my lips as my eyes landed on a familiar pair of gray eyes. My heart seized painfully in a way it hadn't in six years.

When I woke up in an empty bed instead of wrapped in his arms like I had been the night before.

Cody Maxwell had finally returned to Meadowbrook, Montana.

And he was standing in my bar.

He'd been my brother's best friend, the man I'd loved with my whole heart for longer than was smart, and the same man who took my virginity and then left town the next morning without so much as a goodbye. Just a note with two words—*I'm sorry*.

I'd spent too many years wondering if those two words meant he was sorry he'd had sex with me, sorry for leaving, or sorry for something else entirely.

If it wasn't for brief mentions from my brother, Matty —without me ever asking—I'd assume Cody was dead in a ditch somewhere.

The room grew silent as the patrons' gazes darted between Cody and me.

"Hey Mags," he said, his voice that same deep rumble

that had made my stomach pool with desire when I was young and stupid.

You could hear a pin drop, but all I could hear was the rushing of blood in my ears. This was one disappointment too many for today. I wasn't the same weak, lovesick girl he'd left behind six years ago.

"Get out of my bar, Maxwell."

Something sparked in his gaze before determination filled his face. I hated that he was still as handsome as he'd always been. His black hair was shorter than I remembered it—the cut of a man in the military—but his body was bulkier, his muscles prominent where his shirt was tight on his biceps.

"It's a free country," he said, and it took me a second to remember what I'd told him.

I grabbed the coaster back. "Actually, it's not. As the proprietor of this bar, I have the right to refuse service to whoever I want, so I'll repeat myself. Get the fuck out of my bar."

2

CODY

God, she was more beautiful than I remembered and just as fiery as she was when we were kids.

I'd been in love with Maggie Duke for longer than I could remember. I even let myself have her once—a night that had been burned into my brain for six years, accompanied by the heavy guilt of leaving her without a proper goodbye or explanation. I took the coward's way out, and it wasn't something I was proud of. It'd eaten at me since the second I walked away.

I never thought I was good enough for her, but I'd lived enough in the last six years to realize being good enough was a matter of perspective. I didn't think I had much to give her back then, but nearly dying and realizing you never told the woman who held your heart in her hands that she was the love of your fucking life is a pretty big wake-up call.

Maybe I didn't think I was good enough back then, but I knew now with painful certainty that no man would ever love her as fully and completely as I would. As I *did* with every beat of my heart and breath in my body.

But if she thought she could scowl at me and demand I leave and it would work, she was in for a rough time.

I wasn't giving up on a possible future with her, no matter how pissed she got at me.

I settled on my stool and said, "I'll have the IPA on tap."

Fuck, I loved the fire in her eyes. If she were a cartoon, smoke would be billowing out of her ears right about now.

"Clearly your time in the military hasn't made you any smarter. Get out means leave. I won't serve you here."

A giddy rush filled me that she knew I'd been in the military. I hadn't said anything to her before I left, so that meant she must've asked about me while I was gone.

"Well, then I'll sit here and hang out."

"No," she practically growled. Her hazel eyes sparked fire in my veins.

I could still vividly remember the way those eyes had softened during our one night together.

I didn't love that she was trying to look at me with disdain. I probably deserved it, but I didn't like it.

Worse was the faintest bit of hurt in those brown and green eyes. She might have everyone else in this town fooled that she was tough as nails, but I'd seen all her soft sides, and I knew she carried all her hurts down deep where no one else could touch them. But her eyes always gave her away if people would ever take the time to look close enough.

I glanced around at Lyle, Marcus, and Sal. I hadn't seen them in six years and yet they still looked the exact same—weathered old men who fished in the mornings and sat on these stools in the afternoons shooting the shit. They were eyeing me, and instead of the friendly smiles I'd gotten before Maggie had noticed me, their gazes were now filled with suspicion.

It almost made me chuckle, but I was pretty sure if I even cracked a smile, Maggie would flip her lid.

She slapped her palms on the counter and stared me down. "What will it take to get you out of my bar?"

I had a lot of questions about why this bar was hers to begin with. I'd thought she wanted to get out of Meadowbrook and explore the world. Matty had been stingy with the details surrounding why she took over the bar after their dad's accident, but I was determined to get those answers from her as soon as I could.

"Let's start with the IPA on tap and then I'll think about what else I'll need before I leave."

I already knew. I'd been thinking about her and this moment for six fucking years—even more frequently since my last mission went south and I almost died.

But I also knew Maggie. She was stubborn as a mule and needed pushing. So, I'd sit here and push.

Because whether she knew it or not, Maggie Duke owned my heart, and it was time she understood that I was hers and always had been.

3

MAGGIE

The absolute nerve of this motherfucker. Instead of giving him the attitude he was asking for, I spun around on my heels and stormed through the swinging door that separated the front of the bar from the small kitchen. Ben, the cook and a hulking beast of a man, was there setting up the prep for the afternoon and dinner rush. He was my muscle when there was the occasional drunk patron who thought he was above listening to a woman.

And he was just what I needed to kick Cody Maxwell out of my bar.

"Ben, I need your muscle. I've got a patron I need you to remove. He's not welcome here."

He wiped his hands on his towel before tossing it down on the small steel prep table. "Sure thing. Where is he?"

"Sitting next to Lyle."

He nodded and headed out through the swinging door. While part of me wanted to watch Cody's stupid grin get wiped off his still-too-handsome face, I needed a minute to regroup. My heart was beating an erratic pulse in my chest, and my breathing was uneven. But worse was the way my head was a chaotic mess of memories I'd tried so hard to forget.

Cody was my first, and it was a night unlike any other I'd had since. Not that I'd had a lot of men to compare him to, but the three men who briefly kept my bed warm after him were all duds that had me convinced I was better off with a vibrator than the hassle of a man.

The memory of Cody was nothing compared to seeing the man in the flesh, though. I'd been in love with him for most of my life, and my heart had permanent scars from the way he'd left.

I wondered what brought him back to Meadowbrook. His mom had moved to a town about two hours south. Matty still lived in Portland. As far as I was aware, those were the only two people Cody had ever really been close to or cared about. Maybe he was just passing through on his way to see his mom.

I should've been thankful about that prospect—he'd be here and gone in the blink of an eye—but I wasn't.

Apparently it didn't matter how much time passed. My stupid, scarred heart had only ever beat for him.

With a heavy sigh, I faced the door. Ben had probably had enough time to kick Cody out by now.

I walked through and then stopped in my tracks, my eyes blinking, trying to process what I was seeing.

Ben glanced back from his position leaning on the bar, arms crossed and a wide smile on his tan face. He hooked a thumb at Cody. "Why didn't you say it was Maxwell? He's good, Maggie."

My back teeth ground together as I shot a glare at Cody. "You know Ben?"

"Ben played football for Stevensville."

I knew that.

Cody's brow arched. "Your brother played against him, but we all come from small towns, and Stevensville isn't that far so we'd run into him from time to time at bonfires."

"Yeah, Maxwell and I go way back," Ben added, not helpfully.

I closed my eyes and breathed through my nose. I could handle this. I wasn't a naive eighteen-year-old girl anymore, and I wasn't going to let Cody ruin my business. I'd simply pretend he didn't exist—shouldn't be hard since I'd been doing that for six years.

Ignoring Cody turned out to be easier said than done. The problem with small towns, especially Meadowbrook, was that they were filled with nosy busybodies who couldn't help but wander over and say hi when they saw the prodigal son had returned. For the next several hours, as more of my regulars came in, I ended up inundated with comments by folks who clearly could not read the room.

"Oh Maggie, do you remember that one time Matty and Cody climbed that tree off Mullen to save the cat?"

"Maggie, remember that amazing parade float Cody and Matty made during the Fourth of July celebration?"

"Oh, or that one time when Cody and Matty got

caught in that nasty thunderstorm when they were floating on the river and ended up rescuing the Barton girl. You remember that, don't you, Maggie?"

I prided myself on having nerves of steel, but they were a frazzled mess by the time nine o'clock rolled around and James Barton—the Barton girl they'd mentioned before was his sister Ginny—came in to relieve me. He was the only other employee I had besides Ben, but I was happy to have him. When my dad had been running things, he'd been doing almost all of it himself. Back then it had just been a bar with no menu, even though the kitchen setup was always there. When I took over, I hired Ben and James so I wouldn't run myself into the ground the same way my dad had and added a couple of food items. I'd hoped by now to officially make this place a bar and restaurant, but that was another dream down the pipeline.

Right now I was more thankful than ever that I'd hired employees because it meant I could finally get away from Cody Maxwell and enjoy the rest of my Friday night in peace.

Until I walked out the back door and found him leaning against the side of my truck.

"How—" I stammered.

"You didn't think you'd get to escape that easily, did you?"

All my anger fell through my body like a weight dropped at my feet. "Is this some kind of game to you?"

The small smile he'd had on his face evaporated as he

stood tall and closed the short distance between us. "No, Maggie. You were never a game."

"Then what was I?" I asked, my voice a choked whisper. After hours of having him sit right in front of me, I didn't have the energy for this.

He brushed a strand of my brown hair that had fallen out of my messy bun away from my face. "You were my lifeline, my reason for existing."

I scoffed. "Don't bullshit me, Cody. If this is some ploy to get me back in your bed because you want to relive some lame night that happened six years ago, you're wasting your breath." I ignored the pain that slashed across his face at my words. "I don't need you."

It was the same lie I'd been telling myself since I woke up alone that morning.

"Maybe not, but I need you, and I'm not going anywhere, Maggie."

4

CODY

She was pricklier than I remembered—and no one would accuse Maggie Duke of being soft. She'd had a chip on her shoulder since her mom bailed on their family when she was eleven. Marissa Duke had dropped her kids off at school and then driven off into the sunset. She'd left a letter on the kitchen counter saying she'd given up enough of her dreams and was sick of not putting herself first. Matty was thirteen and spent a year trying to find her. Maggie had folded in on herself, becoming quiet and reserved—especially when the rumors swirled around about all the reasons Marissa had left. I'd caught her crying once when I was staying over at their house. Matty and I had been playing outside, and when he ran in to get us some sodas, I walked by the old barn they had behind their house and found Maggie tucked into a ball between two bales of hay. She was silent as a mouse, but her eyes were red-rimmed and tears flowed endlessly down her face. She tried to wipe them away, but I'd already seen them.

There were only a handful of people Maggie ever let see her cry, which was probably why so many people in town thought she wasn't very emotional for a girl. But I knew the truth. Maggie felt everything; she just never let it show.

The fact she was so prickly now made me wonder if life had been harder on her than I'd imagined. I'd made a lot of excuses to myself about why I left her the way I did —that I wasn't good enough, that her brother would take care of her, that she'd fall in love with someone who deserved her big heart, that she'd get out of this small town and live the big life she'd always talked about.

But I was starting to realize that life dealt her a different set of cards than I'd always pictured.

Which meant I had more to make up for than I'd thought, but I'd do it. I'd make up for my mistake. I wasn't leaving her this time. I'd be what she needed because I'd been through my own shit and knew what life was like without her. It wasn't something I wanted to relive. I'd already been forced to wait longer than I would've liked. If it had been up to me, the second I was back on US soil after that shit show of a mission overseas, I would've been on her doorstep.

But I'd had to wait until my leave was approved. I had another three months on my contract before I could be honorably discharged, but I hadn't been able to wait any longer to see her.

"What do you want, Cody?" she asked, her shoulders

drooping and a bone-deep exhaustion seeping out of her body.

"You," I said simply and honestly. She was the only thing I wanted, and I'd take her however I could get her. But I hoped more than anything she'd let me put a ring on her finger and give her the whole fucking world.

Her expression shifted, her walls coming down. Maybe she thought I couldn't see her well in the dark, but I'd made a study of her during all the years I'd been her brother's best friend. I'd also spent the last six years remembering every minor detail about her.

She didn't get teary-eyed—that wasn't Maggie's style —but she did look sad.

Looking down at the ground, she asked, "How long are you in town for?"

"I'm in town for the weekend." She wasn't ready for me to tell her that I had plans to move back after my discharge was processed. She also wasn't ready for me to tell her that she was all I needed to be happy, which was something it had taken me far too long to figure out.

5

MAGGIE

Of course he was only in town for the weekend. That was fitting since he never stayed. Not when I wanted him to. Apparently, he didn't leave when I wanted him to either.

I shouldn't want him to stay now, but standing here across from him—so close I could smell the same sandal-wood cologne he'd worn since high school—I suddenly wanted him to stay. I wished that for once I could have one of my dreams come true and that I wouldn't, once again, be the one left behind. This time, I could do the leaving by putting a time limit on it.

"Where are you staying?"

"Beverly's," he said.

Beverly's Bed and Breakfast was a staple in Meadow-brook. It was the nicest place to stay in town and Beverly was a grandmother to all of us, whether we needed her or not. She knew everything about everyone, but she was pretty good at keeping secrets. She managed to be the town busybody without actually being the town gossip. That was reserved for Ruth Thompson.

"I'm in one of the cottage houses," he added.

Bev had five guest rooms in the main house and three small cottage houses on the property for couples who wanted a bit more privacy.

He was only here for the weekend. At least I knew what to expect. I wouldn't be surprised this time when he disappeared. I'd accepted the fact that I was apparently an easy person to leave behind, so it shouldn't have hurt so much that he was only here for a blip of time.

One weekend.

One weekend in Montana and then he'd be off on his next adventure.

And I'd still be here, right where everyone left me. God, I was sick of people walking away from me like it was nothing.

As I stood across from him, an insane thought popped into my head. What if I could have him for one more night—one more weekend, rather? Maybe one weekend was exactly what I needed to get the closure I'd always thought I deserved. I could scratch the itch that had been growing since the last guy I'd hooked up with two years ago and get Cody Maxwell out of my system for good. More importantly, it would be *my* choice that it was ending. I could be the one to walk away this time.

It was probably a terrible idea, but I figured if I knew there was an expiration date, maybe it would make it easier to wake up alone again.

Standing here across from him was like reliving the greatest night of my life and the worst morning of it.

I'd faced a lot of defeat in my life, a lot of disappointment, but none had burned quite the same way as waking up without Cody Maxwell next to me after he'd made me feel like his whole world for one night.

I should've hated him.

I should've hated the way he left me without a word, for the silence that I'd suffered for six years.

I should have, but I didn't.

Instead, I wanted to chase away the memory from six years ago with a new one—one where I was in control, where I had a say about how this ended, where I knew going in exactly what I was getting.

I'd accepted a long time ago that Cody wasn't my happily ever after, no matter how many years I spent in love with him. But I also couldn't deny that in the one night we'd had, he'd made my body come alive more than any other man I'd been with since.

Something I both loved and hated about Cody was his ability to sit and wait me out. And that's exactly what he was doing. He stood there staring at me, watching me with that serious expression that had always made me feel like he could see right through me to my very soul.

"So, what? You want one weekend with me?" I asked him.

The muscle in his jaw tightened as if he was grinding on his back teeth. "For a start," he said.

I scoffed.

I wasn't that naive eighteen-year-old girl anymore. I knew how the world worked.

"Let's not pretend this is anything more than it is," I told him. "One weekend and I can get you out of my system for good."

His eyes narrowed. "If you think that's possible, then you're a stronger person than I am." He took a step toward me. "Because I haven't been able to get you out of my system my entire life, and I don't ever want to try."

I crossed my arms in front of my chest, my heart beating rapidly and my mind going in a million different directions. But I tamped them all down and focused on the one that was the most obvious, the most possible.

"You got my hopes up once before. Let's just be straight with each other this time. We're both adults. It's just sex. It doesn't have to mean anything."

He stepped forward again and then another step until the toes of his boots were touching mine.

He cupped my cheek, his thumb rubbing softly against my skin, and it took everything in me not to close my eyes and relish the feel of his touch.

How long had it been since someone touched me like this? Like I was precious and worthy and important. A touch that wasn't just a hug from a girlfriend in greeting or my dad patting me on the back because he was proud of me, but a touch because I was *wanted*.

"If you think that I haven't thought about that night every day since, you're delusional. And I don't think you're delusional, Maggie Duke. I think you're one of the smartest, bravest women I've ever known. If you want to pretend this is one weekend of just sex, then I'm gonna take that to mean I have one weekend to prove otherwise."

6

CODY

If she needed to justify in her mind that this was only a weekend-long fling, I'd let her—for now. It was a way in, and I knew as stubborn as Maggie was, I needed whatever way in I could get.

But I also wasn't going to hide my intentions. I'd done that most of my life with her. I was done pretending she didn't own every single piece of me, just like she always had.

Maybe if things had happened differently, I would still have my head shoved up my ass, but nearly dying has a way of forcing you to figure out your priorities.

And the only thing I thought of when I was stuck in that hole with most of my unit already dead was Maggie and that I never told her I loved her.

I wouldn't repeat my past mistake.

By the end of this weekend, she'd know. All my cards would be laid out, and she'd decide if I was good enough for her.

"I'll follow you," she said before pushing past me, opening her truck door, and hopping in.

I couldn't believe she was still driving that old thing.

She didn't give me any time to answer before she was starting her truck and arching her brown brows at me. I walked around the side of the building where I'd parked my rental, and when I saw her headlights behind me, I took off to Beverly's.

The drive was quick. Everything in this town was within a ten-to-fifteen-minute drive. Beverly's was on the edge of town where she had a large plot of land for the B&B and the additional cottages.

About a block away from Beverly's, her headlights disappeared from behind me as she took a right down a side street. I carried on, driving down the gravel road to the cottage I was staying in, and sat in my rental car, wondering if she was going to come back or if she'd changed her mind. I moved to the porch and sat on one of the chairs there, barely feeling the chill in the air as I waited. Disappointment swirled in my gut at the thought that she wouldn't show. I knew I deserved it, but I'd already been apart from her for far longer than I liked. I didn't relish the thought of wasting any more time.

A half hour passed before headlights came down the road and her old truck parked next to mine.

But she didn't get out of the truck right away. From the ambient light coming off the porch light of the cottage, I could see her looking at the other cottages— both vacant, or else I was sure she'd turn right around and leave.

Trepidation crossed her face for the briefest moment before she tilted her chin up and turned off the truck. She got out and walked toward me, her steps sure, her eyes trained on mine.

"I thought maybe you'd changed your mind."

"Thought about it," she said, looking all around the outside of the cottage and avoiding my gaze. "After all, last time we played this game, you made me wait."

It wasn't a game—it never had been, but all I could do now was prove myself to her and prove that our connection had been real all those years ago and was just as real now.

She arched her brow as she looked at me. "Well? Are we going in or did you plan to try to seduce me outside?"

I couldn't hold back my smile if I tried. Fuck, I loved her. I loved her sass. I loved her false confidence when I knew she was worried about people finding out about this and what they'd say—small towns like ours thrived on gossip. I loved that fire in her eyes that matched the challenge in her words.

I loved her, whether she was busting my balls or flushed and panting from her release—a visual that had kept my hand busy during our time apart, especially since in all these years, I'd refused to fuck anyone else. My body belonged to Maggie Duke—whether she knew it or not—and it would've been cheating as far as I was concerned to be with anyone else.

I tried not to think about how many guys she'd probably been with since our night together. I didn't judge her or fault her for attempting to move on because she didn't know that I'd been hers all along.

Without further ado, I opened the door and gestured for her to go first.

She finally looked up at me, those beautiful hazel eyes of hers giving away how she really felt. Her eyes had always been her giveaway, and right now they were filled with a mix of fear and longing—telling me she was scared of this, of me hurting her again, but she also wanted me as badly as I wanted her.

She dropped her gaze and my stomach clenched. Before I could think it through, I wrapped my hand around the side of her neck, my thumb gently applying pressure to her chin so she'd lift her face to mine. Those big eyes met mine again, and my body responded instantly.

"I'll do whatever it takes to keep you this time," I murmured before I crashed my lips down on hers and sealed my promise with a kiss.

7

MAGGIE

His kiss had the same effect on me as it had all those years ago. I both hated and loved it. Hated it because he was the only man who'd ever made me feel like this and loved it because it was the only time I ever felt like I got to be soft.

Cody had always seemed to know what I needed without me telling him. He would take control, and for once in my life I could let everything go. I could let someone else carry the weight that constantly sat on my shoulders.

Even knowing he'd broken my heart once before didn't stop my body from responding to him. I never figured out what it was about him—and whatever it was clearly hadn't changed—that always made me feel safe in his arms. Even when I'd fallen off my bike and skinned my knees badly, I'd felt safer than I'd ever remembered feeling with his arms wrapped around me as my brother ran to get our dad. Even after the way he left me and with the hurt I still felt whenever I remembered the morning after our night together, I felt safe with his arms around me.

And this kind of safety wasn't something I'd felt since that night. So I gave in.

I melted into him.

His hand tightened on the side of my neck as the other wrapped around my waist, hauling me against his hard body. His tongue licked across the seam of my lips, and I parted them on a gasp as every nerve ending in my body seemed to spark to life. He groaned as he got his first taste, and his kiss turned ravenous.

I was lost in the feel of him, the way my heart raced in my chest, the throbbing pulse of desire between my legs, the tight knot of nerves in my stomach. Was this a mistake? Would I come to regret this moment, even if it felt *so damn good* to let go?

"I've got you, Mags. I've got you," he murmured against my lips, and I ignored the voice filled with fear whispering in the back of my mind that Cody Maxwell was a one-way ticket to heartbreak.

I'd be forced to accept the consequences of my actions once he left, but for now I wasn't going to think about that. I wanted to feel good, no matter how temporary.

I didn't want to fight it. I craved the excuse to let my guard down and let him make me feel things I'd long forgotten.

I nodded my head to his statement because my voice

was stuck in my throat. He kissed me again harder as he carried me into the cottage.

Once inside, his hands slid down my body to the edge of my shirt. He broke the kiss again, both of us panting, and his heated gaze held me captive as he lifted my shirt off, discarding it on the floor. His chest heaved as his hungry gaze devoured my body in just my bra and jeans. It wasn't the sexiest bra I'd ever worn—just plain white cotton—but the way he looked at me made me feel like it was the sexiest lingerie in the world.

His large hands moved to the button on my jeans, and I sucked in a quiet breath as he popped the button and then slid down the zipper, slowly, like he wanted to savor every second of undressing me. He pushed my jeans down, then got down on his knees before me, delicately slipping off my shoes and socks, and then removing my pants the rest of the way.

I think I forgot to breathe because I got lightheaded as I watched him trace my long legs with his gaze before he followed the same path with his fingertips. My eyes closed at the sensation of his fingers sliding over my smooth skin. His touch was soft, but his hands were clearly the hands of a man who worked hard—there was nothing soft about them.

"I've dreamt of this moment," he whispered like he was confessing, and I suppose he was. "Every night, I closed my eyes and went back to that night in the cabin, the feel of your skin, your touch." His gaze had that hungry look again when he met mine. "The way this tight pussy gripped me like it was the only place I belonged in the world."

I swallowed thickly, at a complete loss for words.

He didn't look away as his finger brushed between my legs over my underwear, no doubt feeling how wet I already was. He groaned. "Fuck, Maggie. You're so wet for me, aren't you, baby?"

All I could do was nod. A riot of confusing emotions swirled inside me, and I was afraid if I spoke I might do something stupid like tell him to stop when that was the last thing I wanted. I was already more turned on than I'd been in years.

A moment of conflict passed across his face, like he wanted to say something but wasn't sure if he should.

"What?" I asked, my voice hoarse with desire.

He gripped the waist of my underwear and pulled them down my legs and off to join the rest of my clothes. He returned his finger between my legs, this time gently pushing it inside. We both moaned at the touch.

I forgot I'd even asked him a question when he finally spoke, his own voice husky and thick. "This is the only place I belong, which is why there hasn't been anyone else."

It took a second for the words to penetrate the fog of lust I was under, and to understand why he said it like he was afraid this might scare me off. Maybe if he wasn't touching me, it would've. But with his thick finger inside me and his thumb rubbing teasing circles over my clit, all I could do was acknowledge the way his words made my chest ache with all the things I'd wanted six years ago.

"You're not ready to hear everything I need to say to you, Maggie, but I need you to know, there's been no one since you. You've owned every piece of me since that night in the cabin."

Words built in my throat, but before any of them could be unleashed, he lifted my leg over his shoulder and leaned forward, licking the seam of my pussy before swirling his wicked tongue over my clit. A moan escaped as I gripped his head and held him against me. My legs trembled as the pleasure built rapidly. When he added his fingers into the mix again, I knew I wouldn't last long. Pleasure coiled tight in my belly as my hips started rocking against his mouth, seeking the release I knew he could give me.

He groaned against my clit and then sucked hard as his fingers curled inside me, and I came on a shout, my whole body shaking from the intensity of my orgasm. He placed a kiss on the landing strip I'd fortunately had rewaxed recently, and then swept me off my feet and carried me to the bed. He placed me down gently, like I was precious, and emotion clogged my throat.

I'd forgotten it could feel like *this*. Like it wasn't just scratching an itch and then getting dressed and leaving, but that I could feel treasured, and that my pleasure seemed just as important to my partner as his own.

He stripped out of his clothes, his gaze locked on mine the whole time. Neither of us said a word, but the air was thick with everything we weren't saying. The hurt, the longing, the need.

I felt like Cody could see right to my very soul when he looked at me like that.

He pulled a condom out of a box in his duffel bag, and I arched a questioning brow at him. The right side of his mouth tilted up into a boyish grin that I didn't want to find adorable, but did. "I was hopeful."

And then the grin slipped off his face as he crawled over my body. When his eyes met mine again, it seemed like he was checking in, making sure this was still what I wanted. I nodded and he guided his thick length between my legs. He slid inside me slowly—achingly slow.

"Goddamn, you feel so fucking good. It's been a long time, so I apologize now if I don't last long."

My lips pulled up into a small smile as I let out a reluctant giggle.

And then he rocked his hips forward, burying himself to the hilt, and any remaining laughter died on my lips. "Fuck," I muttered.

He grunted as he pulled back, almost all the way out, and then thrust forward again. My fingers dug into his back as my legs tightened around his hips, my body naturally rocking in time with his thrusts. He was so thick and the stretch was right on the edge of too much, but it also felt so fucking good, I never wanted him to stop. His cock hit pleasure points inside of me I'd forgotten I even had.

My stomach tightened as the flutter of another orgasm was felt between my legs. How long had it been since I'd had more than one with a partner?

"Fuck, baby. Do that again and I'm gonna come. Goddamn, you're fucking tight."

"Don't stop," I begged, my voice throaty and deep as my whole body seemed to ignite in pleasure. He couldn't stop now when I was so close. Just a little more...

He picked up the pace of his thrusts, his face tight with concentration, and I could tell he was doing everything in his power to hold back his orgasm until I came again. His neck muscles bulged with his restraint and then he moved his hand between us and started rubbing circles on my clit.

I came with a scream, my body convulsing, my legs tightening on his hips as I rode through the most powerful orgasm I'd ever had in my life. Cody was right there with me, his body tight as he shook through his climax.

He dropped his weight on top of me, but I didn't mind. His sweaty skin against mine eased whatever panic I might normally have felt after experiencing something as mind-blowing as that.

After a few minutes, he let out a heavy breath and rolled off me, but only long enough to pull off the condom and throw it in the small trash can on the other side of the nightstand. Then he pulled the comforter over our bodies and pulled me against him, my back to his front. He nuzzled against my neck. "Let's take a nap before round two."

8

CODY

Maggie Duke was in my bed.

No matter how many times I told myself it was real, it felt like a dream. I knew a freak-out from her was imminent. Maggie was used to people letting her down, and unfortunately, that was something I'd already done once before, so I didn't exactly have the best track record.

She was lying on her stomach, one arm under the pillow, the other across my chest. Her brown hair fell in messy waves around her face. Her mouth was slightly parted, and her face looked the most peaceful I'd seen it since I returned to town.

Watching her sleep, I couldn't help thinking about how different this time was compared to last time when I could barely stomach looking at her because I knew I had to leave. I'd been afraid if I looked at her, I wouldn't be able to walk out the door.

Maggie had always made me want to stay, but I'd convinced myself I needed to prove my worth.

I traced the smooth skin of her shoulder, then over the few tattoos she had—the outline of a mountain range with 406 in it, an eagle, and a shooting star. It'd been too dark last night to see the details of her tattoos—which is how I also knew she hadn't been able to see the detail of mine. I knew she'd know what it meant as soon as she saw it.

Her phone started buzzing on the nightstand and then made a high-pitched ringing. Maggie groaned and buried her head in the pillow. "Nooo. Just a few more minutes."

This was a new side to her I hadn't seen. Apparently my girl wasn't a morning person. I chuckled and she stiffened, lifting her head abruptly and squinting her eyes against the bright morning light. She blinked at me a few times and then whispered, "Am I still dreaming?"

My smile fell as my chest tightened. "No, baby, you're not."

She was frozen for a minute before she rolled over, taking the sheet with her and keeping herself covered up. "Uh, I need to go to work," she said, still facing away from me.

"The bar is open at nine a.m.?"

"No, but I have inventory and shit I need to deal with. There's a lot more to running a business than just opening and closing."

I let out a sigh as my head fell back on the pillow. She was back to being prickly, which meant she still felt she needed to protect herself from me. I thought we'd made headway last night, but apparently we still had a ways to go. I resigned myself to giving her the space she needed, but that didn't mean I was giving up. It was only Saturday, which meant I still had all day tomorrow to convince her to give me another chance and hopefully come back to Georgia with me.

She quickly got dressed, and I watched her, my body tense as I fought against the urge to wrap my hands around her waist and pull her back to bed. That wouldn't be received well right now. So I let her go, and after she raced out of the cottage without a backward glance, I decided today would be a good day to get some other things in order.

Maggie wasn't the only part of my future I was ready for.

9

MAGGIE

The words on the inventory page in front of me blurred as my vision zoned out for the fifth time.

"Ugh," I grumbled.

I couldn't focus because all I kept thinking about was Cody. Why did he have to come back? Especially now.

I could pretend I was doing so well without him when he wasn't here.

But now that he'd waltzed back into my life, there was no denying how cold I'd felt over the last six years without him. He was a ray of sunshine and seemed to be the only thing that could warm me.

Which was really inconvenient, considering he'd already told me he was only here for the weekend.

Maybe "inconvenient" wasn't the right word. It was downright stupid. Because I knew the only thing Cody was capable of giving me was heartbreak.

Well, that and orgasms. But would they really be

worth it when he'd devastate me when he left on Monday morning?

My phone buzzed beside me, and with trepidation, I glanced at it, worried it might be Cody. But that worry was apparently pointless, because instead it was my best friend, Joni, texting me that she was outside and to let her in.

I pushed up from my desk and walked through the quiet, empty bar. Sometimes I didn't mind the quiet early mornings when I had to come in and do admin tasks. But I preferred when there was a crowd. It was much easier to ignore my thoughts when I was surrounded by people and busy running things.

I swung the door open to find Joni standing on the other side, her hands full with two cups of coffee from our favorite local coffee shop, Grizzly Grounds. My shoulders sagged with relief, and a smile lifted the corners of my lips as I reached out and grabbed my coffee.

"How'd you know?" I asked her.

"While I was getting gas this morning, I overheard Gunther Novak talking about how he saw Cody Maxwell at the bar last night. So I figured you would need a pick-me-up. Wanna talk about it?"

"No," I said, but she knew I'd talk to her anyway.

Joni Sanders and Savannah Richards had been my best friends since kindergarten, but despite being my best friends, I had never told them that I lost my virginity to Cody. They knew I'd had a horrendous crush on him my entire life, but that's all they thought it was. They didn't know the true devastation that he'd wreaked on me when he left. Although I was pretty sure Joni suspected. She had a sixth sense about these kinds of things.

She followed me back to my office and took the seat on the other side of my desk and waited for me to take a long drink of my hot vanilla latte.

She arched a brow. "Well?"

"Well, what?"

She rolled her eyes. "Don't give me that. You know exactly what. Cody Maxwell's here and he sat at your bar all night long. Everyone's talking about it. You're gonna sit there and tell me you're not feeling some kind of way about that?"

I took another sip of my coffee trying to buy myself time, but I knew it was a losing battle.

Then with a shift of her gaze to the side, she took a sip of her own coffee and dropped a bomb. "Or I suppose I could just believe the rumors that your truck was seen outside one of Beverly's cottages where Mr. Maxwell himself is rumored to be staying."

I sagged back against my chair. "Fuck, I hate living in a small town. There's no semblance of privacy here."

"Well, we could have pretended that you told me all these things if you had just, you know, spilled the beans. It's not my fault we live in a small town with a bunch of chatty people who have nothing better to do than talk about a prodigal son's unexpected return to town."

"So..." she added when I didn't say anything, lost in thought as I stared out the window.

For her to understand the true turmoil of what I was feeling, I was going to have to tell her the full story, and a part of me felt guilty that I'd never told her any of this before. But I'd been eighteen—young and heartbroken—and that night with Cody had been the only thing that belonged to me and me alone. Keeping that secret to myself had made it easier to avoid the burn in my chest when I thought about how I'd woken up alone. It made it easier to focus on the positive moments of that night. The way he'd held me close, how gentle he'd been with me, even though he hadn't known that I was a virgin.

"I was with Cody last night."

She squealed. "Oh my gosh, I knew it."

But then she saw my face and her smile of joy fell. "Wait, was he horribly bad in bed? Oh my God, the whole buildup of wanting him for this long. I mean, you've crushed on him forever and then you finally get with him and it's awful?"

I covered my face with my hands and leaned on my desk. "Do you remember the night before he skipped town? The night I left the bonfire by the river early and you had to get a ride with Sav and Wes?"

"Yes," she said, dragging out the word.

"Cody and I went up to the cabin and had sex that night," I said in a rush.

Her jaw dropped, and it would have been comical if I wasn't feeling like such a shitty friend for keeping this secret from her.

"Holy shit," she whispered. "Are you serious right now?"

"Uh, yeah."

"Why didn't you ever tell me?" Before I could answer, her eyes went wide. "Oh my God. And then he left the next morning." Sadness filled her gaze. "Oh Maggie, you must have been devastated. Why wouldn't you tell us that? Sav and I would have been by your side in a heartbeat. We would have helped you with whatever you needed, whether it was eating your weight in ice cream and pizza or railing at the universe that he even existed. You didn't have to go through that alone."

I loved her all the more for saying it even though she didn't have to. This was why she and Sav were my best friends.

"I wanted him to be my secret," I confessed. "I wanted him to be just mine. If I told anyone—"

She cut me off as understanding filled her face. "It wouldn't be *yours* anymore."

"Right," I said.

"So what was it like seeing him last night?"

"Weird and painful and wonderful." I added the last word with a heavy sigh.

It made me feel weak to say it—and there was nothing I hated more than feeling weak—but it was the truth. No one had ever made me feel as safe and free as Cody Maxwell did when he had me wrapped in his arms, which felt outrageous considering he was the one who had broken my heart worse than anyone else. But it didn't change how I felt around him.

I told Joni about our night together, his plans for only being here for the weekend, and how I had convinced myself that I could do a weekend fling and I'd be fine because I was Maggie fucking Duke and if I couldn't handle a one-night stand, or a one-weekend stand as it was, then I wasn't as strong as I thought I was.

Joni did not seem to think it was as good of an idea as I did.

"Are you sure about this?" she asked. "I don't want to see you devastated come Monday morning when he's gone."

I didn't want that either. But I'd already opened this can of worms and now that I'd had him again, I wanted every minute I could get, even if I knew there was an expiration at the end of it.

Even if just the thought of it ending already made my heart twinge in my chest.

10

CODY

I'd forgotten how beautiful the drive was along highway 93 from the Bitterroot toward CFU—Clark Fork University. It was a forty-five-minute drive because traffic in these parts was usually light, and I chose to use the time to call Matty, Maggie's brother.

He and I didn't talk as often as we should have, but he was still my best friend and he knew more than most. Except there was one big secret I had kept from him, and he needed to hear it from me.

The phone rang three times before he answered. "Hey man, what's up?"

"Hey, I just wanted to give you a call. I'm in Montana."

"No way. Are you heading back to Meadowbrook? Or are you visiting your mom?"

My mom had moved several hours away from where we'd once lived in Meadowbrook.

"No, not seeing my mom this time. I'm...well,"—I let

out a heavy gust of air—"I'm in Meadowbrook to convince your sister to marry me."

He choked across the line but I kept barreling through.

"Well, not marry me because I don't think she'd say yes after a weekend, but that is the long game. I'm in love with your sister and have been for probably close to a decade. She's always been the only woman I wanted, and I didn't tell you because I didn't want you to beat the shit out of me. I didn't even think I deserved her but I know better now. After what happened overseas, I just kept picturing dying in that desert and her never knowing what she meant to me, and I couldn't stomach the thought. So now I'm here and I want her in my life."

The only noise in the cab of my rental car was the sound of the wheels on the highway and the static of the phone call.

"Matty?"

"You're seriously in love with my sister?"

"Yeah." I held my breath, waiting for him to rip me a new one.

"Why the fuck would you think I wouldn't approve? You're my best friend. I wouldn't be friends with you if I didn't think you were a good guy."

My shoulders sagged as all the stress I'd carried for far too long faded away. I didn't realize how much I needed to hear that from him until this moment.

"You said you've been in love with her for close to a decade?" he asked. "So you had a crush on my sister when we were in high school?"

"Okay, maybe more like eight years. I liked her for a few years before anything ever happened."

"Whoa, whoa, whoa," he said. "Are you saying something happened between you back then?"

I told him about the bonfire six years earlier when we were twenty and she was eighteen, and my night with her—minus the details because it was his sister—then the shitty way I left with only a note telling her I was sorry.

"Okay, well now I'm pissed at you," he said. "I definitely would have beat your ass if I'd known that."

That brought a chuckle out of me. "Good to know."

"But you're back for her now," he confirmed.

"Yeah, I am."

"Does she know your plan?" he asked.

"Not yet." I wasn't sure she was ready for it. "She's a little prickly about our whole situation. I think the only reason she gave me the time of day this time is because she thinks I'm only here for the weekend."

"Sounds about right."

I could practically see him nodding through the phone.

"I'm done sitting on the sidelines of her life," I told him.

I was already nearing the university, so I knew we'd need to hang up soon, and I didn't want there to be any questions about how devoted I was to this plan.

"I'm glad you finally went after her," he said softly. "You were always good enough for her. You were the only one who thought you weren't. You've always been a stand-up guy, and you deserve to be happy. So does my sister."

My throat was tight with emotion. "Thanks, man."

He hummed. "I've always felt guilty for the shit she got stuck with, so I mean it when I say she deserves someone who will fight for her. That said, if you break her heart again, I will come and punch you in the face."

My lips pulled up at the corners. "I would expect no less."

We hung up, and I felt lighter than I had in a long time.

A few minutes later, I walked into the Student Union building where I was meeting with four of my hockey players. It had been a long time since I'd been in this building, but it felt the same as it always had.

I never thought I'd coach hockey. Hell, it had been years since I'd played. But when I got a call from Drew Dumontier—who I'd coached when I was in high school and he was just in the local kids' league—I knew I couldn't pass up the opportunity. I loved hockey and I was excited to take my passion for the sport to the next level.

CFU wasn't big enough for NCAA Division Hockey, so it was club hockey, but from what Drew had explained over the phone, they had a solid fan base and the team had worked hard on their skills. Their captain, Foster Kane, was particularly invested in making sure the program was solid before he graduated in two years. It was a good thing they were talented since club hockey often left it up to the players to get funding for uniforms, equipment, games, and even hiring the coach.

I spotted Drew first as I walked into the student-run café. Three other guys sat at the table, one of which I recognized as Liam Farrell—another kid I'd coached back in the day. He and Drew had practically been glued at the hip, and it appeared that hadn't changed.

Drew stood when he caught sight of me. "Hey Cody," he said, extending his hand. "It's good to see you again."

"You too." He definitely wasn't the scrawny twelve-year-old I used to coach.

The other guys had stood once Drew did. The tall brown-haired one extended his hand. "Foster Kane. Thanks for agreeing to be our coach. You obviously know Drew, and probably Liam. This is Harrison Gordon," he said, pointing to the two other guys, and I shook their hands as well.

"But we all call him Gordy," Liam said.

"Nice to see you again, Liam," I said with a smile.

"You too, Cody."

Foster was starting his junior year but already carried himself like a leader, and it was clear the other guys looked up to him just in the way they already deferred to him. I had a good feeling about him as captain and suspected he wouldn't be one to let his ego get in the way of my coaching.

"We really appreciate you stepping up to do this, especially after our last coach quit with such short notice," Liam said.

"Happy to do it. I'm moving back to the area anyway, so it gives me something to do."

The pay wasn't great. Frankly, it was kind of garbage, but it gave me an excuse to stay close to Maggie and do something I enjoyed, which was really all I cared about.

Foster slid a thick folder my way. "What's this?" I asked.

"Your contract, club rules, student athlete expectations for the university, our current game schedule, and some other miscellaneous things I thought you might find helpful."

I opened the folder to look through the documents while Foster continued. "We need to do some major fundraising this year. Several of our uniforms are getting worn out, and Gordy, who's our goalie, needs better pads. So we're hoping we can raise a decent amount of money so that our guys don't have to pay for it out of our own pockets."

These boys seemed like they had good ideas, good instincts. The information in the packet was more thorough than Foster had made it sound. He was organized and on top of things. I was surprised he was only six years younger than I was.

I looked around the table and was impressed with how focused they were on this meeting. It was clear they wanted this, which was a lot more effort than I expected for club hockey.

These guys weren't playing so they could go pro. They were playing because this was their last chance to play a game they loved before they had to go live life, work on the family farm or ranch, join their dad's business, or make their own way in the world.

No matter what their path post college would be, everyone at this table knew hockey would be something on the side, if they even got that lucky. This was their last chance to play it the way they wanted to.

"Alright, so let's talk it out," I said.

We spent the next several hours going over all the information in the packet, their plans for this year, and how they wanted to grow the club. Foster and Harrison were juniors while Liam and Drew were sophomores. They still had some time, but they wanted to build a program that would carry a legacy beyond them, and I was all for helping them out.

Because I was all too aware of how important a legacy was, and I was eager to leave my own mark, especially if it meant firming up my roots in Montana.

After grabbing dinner and driving past the bar, I headed for Maggie's place. When I'd seen Maggie's face through the window of Duke's, I'd decided to let her stew a little longer in the hopes it would move things along. A quick text to Matty got me her address. I was surprised to find out she was living in the converted apartment above her dad's garage.

The house looked the same as I remembered it—a little weathered, but overall well-maintained. Knowing what I knew now, I wondered how much of the maintenance fell on Maggie since her dad's health had declined. In front of the garage was clear, so I parked in one of the two spots available, then got out and walked over to the stairs that led up to Maggie's apartment. It was a nice enough night out, although chilly.

Inhaling deeply, I closed my eyes and let the weight on my shoulders fall. There was nothing like breathing the fresh Montana air in your lungs. It was crisp and clean instead of the oppressive heat I still had the occasional nightmare about.

The sound of a door opening pulled me from my reverie, and I opened my eyes to glance over and find Maggie's dad standing at his back door.

Tom Duke had looked a lot better the last time I saw him. He'd always been a tall man with an imposing build, but now he looked frail with his shoulders hunched and his skin slightly sagging. His movements were also more stilted than I remembered.

"Well, I'll be damned. Cody Maxwell returns." His face broke out in a smile that had my own cheeks lifting, and he opened up his arms. "Get over here, son, and give me a hug."

I didn't hesitate. My own father had never been around. Tom Duke had been that father figure for me, and it pained me to realize Maggie wasn't the only person I'd bailed on.

"How are you, Mr. Duke?"

He scoffed. "None of that Mr. Duke nonsense. It's Tom."

He'd been saying that since I was a kid, but my mom

had always reminded me to call him Mr. Duke, so that's what I'd done.

He gripped my shoulder and took a good look at me, his eyes shining with pride. "Matty told me you were a military man."

"Yes, sir."

His hand squeezed my shoulder, but it was nowhere near as strong as it used to be. "I'm proud of you, Cody. You really went out and made something of yourself."

I swallowed hard. If he knew everything—especially how I'd hurt his daughter—he wouldn't be saying that.

"So what brings you back to Meadowbrook?"

My stomach tightened with nerves, but I wouldn't lie to him. "Maggie. I'm here for Maggie."

His gaze bored into me as his brows furrowed in confusion for a brief second. But then the corners of his lips lifted slightly before he shook his head and chuckled. "I wondered when you'd pull your head out of your ass and make a move. Took you long enough."

My jaw dropped and that only made him laugh louder.

"Oh, please. I've got eyes, don't I? My memory might not be as sharp as it used to be, but I still remember how you were when you were younger. How Matty never noticed the way you were always attuned to Maggie is beyond me." His expression sobered. "I don't know what happened between you two before, but you leaving really did a number on her." He raised his hand as I opened my mouth. "I don't need the details, and we all know Maggie is too proud to ever share her feelings with most people, let alone me—she'd probably be mortified if she knew I'd noticed. So we'll keep that between us, but I'd like to know that you aren't planning to up and leave again like last time."

"No, sir. I'm not planning to leave like last time. I'm settling here in Meadowbrook—not right away, but things are already in motion."

He nodded once. "I'm glad to hear that. My daughter is made of sterner stuff than most, but that doesn't mean she can't get her heart broken. I like you, Cody. I've always considered you family. I'd hate for that to change."

His look said it all—if I hurt his daughter again, I'd no longer be welcome here.

"I promise I have no intention of hurting her again. It's hard enough to live with the knowledge that I hurt her the first time."

He clapped me on the back and then turned back toward the door, exhaustion settling across his features. "Glad to hear it. Apologies, Cody, but my energy isn't what it used to be. I gotta go lie down, but don't be a stranger, okay?"

"I won't be," I assured him before watching him take an unsteady step back toward his house.

"Here, let me help," I offered.

His cheeks flushed and anger flashed in his eyes before it disappeared. "I can do it."

He sounded as stubborn as a toddler, and the shift in his demeanor took me aback for a second. I didn't want to see him fall, but I also wasn't sure exactly what was happening, so I let him go and watched carefully as he shuffled inside and closed the back door.

His health was worse than I'd expected and worse than Matty had made it out to be which made me think he might not know how bad it was. Once again, Maggie had been carrying the weight of the world on her shoulders by herself.

It stopped now.

If I had anything to say about it, she'd never have to carry another burden alone for the rest of her life.

I sat down on the stairs and got comfortable as I waited for Maggie to close down the bar.

11

MAGGIE

The seat of the chair thudded heavily on the tabletop as I flipped it over a little harder than I normally would when I closed up.

Okay, maybe a lot harder.

My irritation only grew as the night wore on, and now that all my patrons had left, the neon "open" sign had been turned off, and I was stacking chairs on the tables, it had reached a new level. I was angry at myself that I was disappointed at all, but I could no longer deny that disappointment was at the heart of my irritation.

Cody never came to see me.

He hadn't said he would. In fact, he seemed all for giving me the space I'd requested, but I'd half expected him to show up anyway.

And maybe a stupid, girly part of me had hoped he would—that he'd show me it wasn't just sex, which was especially stupid to want because I was the one who had agreed to this one-weekend-only, just-sex arrangement.

Did I sweep a little more forcefully because I was mad? Yes.

Did I scrub the counters instead of just wiping them off and mutter curse words to myself the whole time? Also yes.

And by the time the bar was all closed up, I was exhausted and still disappointed.

God, I was going to get my heart broken again when he left, wasn't I?

Why couldn't I say no to him? If I just had the strength to say no to him, I could have prevented all of this. But where he was concerned, I had always been weak for him.

Apparently, twenty-four-year-old Maggie wasn't all that different from eighteen-year-old Maggie.

I thought I'd grown and matured. I'd been forced to when my dad's health declined after his traumatic brain injury and I had to take over the bar. But now I still felt like that stupid girl pining for her brother's best friend.

I got in my car and drove home, pretending that there wasn't a ball of emotion building in my throat and that the subtle burn behind my eyes was just because I was tired.

I hadn't gotten enough sleep last night and then I spent all day doing admin tasks and then running the bar all night. I was exhausted. That was the excuse I was going with, because I refused to cry over Cody fucking Maxwell. Not anymore. Those days were supposed to be long behind me.

"If he isn't going to think about me all day, then I'm not going to think about him," I muttered to myself.

I ignored the fact that I had obviously already spent all day thinking about him, so that kind of nullified my whole argument.

I didn't bother driving to Beverly's since I figured Cody was done with whatever this had been.

I lived with my dad in town, not too far from the bar. He had converted the space above the garage into an apartment when I was in high school. I think he'd been hoping my brother would live here, but Matty—he would always be Matty to me, even if he introduced himself as Matt these days—had gotten an incredible job offer in Portland right out of college and moved to follow his career dreams. Honestly, I didn't think he was ever going to come back to Montana. He liked living in a big city, and we didn't really have that here. Our largest and closest city was Missoula, and it was still nowhere near the size of Portland.

While my brother had always had big-city dreams, I'd been content to live in our small town. Sure, I'd had my own dreams of traveling the world and seeing new places, but I always wanted to end up here in Meadowbrook. I loved small-town life, even if it was impossible to have any semblance of privacy in a town our size.

So, when my dad accepted that Matty wouldn't be living in Meadowbrook, he offered the apartment to me. Considering the rent was cheap, and I could still keep an eye on my dad and help him as needed, it seemed like the best of both worlds.

But as I pulled up and saw another familiar vehicle parked in front of the garage, I realized I'd made a huge error. Because if Cody was parked in front of the garage, that meant my dad knew he was in town—and worse, that he was here to see me.

Cody was sitting on the stairs that led up to my apartment, his hands folded in his lap as he relaxed casually and waited for me.

My heart started to race with panic, and I glanced over to the house where my dad lived.

Cody sat up on alert as I focused back on him.

"Did you talk to him?" I asked him. There was no way he could miss the unnaturally high pitch of my voice.

"Yeah," he said.

I closed my eyes and covered them with my hand. God, I was not looking forward to the conversation I was going to have to have with my dad now. He'd always loved Cody. "That probably wasn't a good idea. He'll get his hopes up that you're sticking around."

Cody grinned. "If only you'd have the same hopes."

I dropped my hand. He did not just say that to me. "Are you fucking serious right now?"

Fire seemed to light in his eyes at my attitude.

"What are you even doing here?" I asked him.

His eyes narrowed, but he still had that stupid, satisfied grin on his face. Like he knew why I was so irrationally angry.

"Wipe that stupid smirk off your face. You're not getting laid tonight."

His smirk only grew into a full-blown smile. "You sure about that?"

I practically felt the smoke billowing out of my ears. I could slap that smug look off his face. "You never answered my question. Why are you here?"

He nodded like that deflection was exactly what he was expecting from me. "Because I figured you'd be well and truly pissed right now and your stubbornness would prevent you from coming to me, so I decided to come to you."

"And why should I be pissed at you?" I asked, trying for a nonchalant tone, even though he was one hundred percent right, which only annoyed me further. He wasn't supposed to know me this well after one night together six years ago.

I *was* pissed, even if deep down I knew I didn't have a right to be. We weren't anything serious. This was just supposed to be a fling—a way to get him out of my system once and for all.

"My meeting today took a little longer than I expected."

"What meeting?" I asked.

"Why? You suddenly care?" He arched a brow.

I crossed my arms over my chest. "No. It's none of my business."

He shook his head. "Maggie, when will you realize everything I do is your business? *I* am your business. Make me your fucking business."

My heart was no longer racing out of panic, but

because I didn't know how to respond. Because the truth was I so desperately wanted him to be mine.

I'd wanted him to be mine for as long as I could remember. And he was dangerously close to making me think he really wanted that too.

But I knew him, and he wasn't the guy that would stick around. He hadn't before and he wouldn't now. No one ever stayed for me. Besides, what would he even do here? It's not like jobs were easy to come by around here.

None of that mattered because he had told me himself he was leaving after this weekend. So what were we even doing?

I dropped my arms, my shoulders heavy with defeat. "Maybe this was a bad idea, Cody." Stupid idea, actually, but I felt stupid enough without saying the actual word.

He was in front of me before I even knew what was going on, wrapping his hand around the back of my neck and his gaze boring into mine, our breaths mingling in the chilly spring air. "Why is it a bad idea?" he asked.

I'd never realized how terrifying it was to be brave, but right now I felt the need to be well and truly brave the first time in my life.

As I looked into the eyes of the man who I'd always been in love with, I told him the truth. "Because I don't think I can have casual with you, Cody. I don't think one weekend was ever going to be enough to scratch the itch. I spent all day becoming a raging bitch and irrationally angry when I thought that you just weren't interested anymore. That's not the person I want to be. That's not the woman I *am*. I don't want to be the girl who waits around for you anymore. So just let me go."

He took the one step closer until his body was flush against mine. "I'm never letting you go. Letting you go before is the one and only real mistake I have ever made in my entire life, and I've spent every second since regretting it. I learned that life is short, and I'm not willing to have that regret hanging over my head any longer. I love you, Maggie. I have loved you every moment since the first minute that I really, really saw you when I was eighteen. You are the only one I want." He dipped his head closer, his voice deep and intimate. "This was never going to be one weekend."

"But," I started, but he sealed his lips over mine before any other words could form. Any questions or concerns I was about to raise completely cleared from my head as I melted against him, letting him kiss me senseless. All I could think about was the feel of his lips on mine, the way he held me tight to his body like he was afraid of losing me.

And I gave in because I wanted him too.

I'd always wanted him.

12

CODY

My mouth plundered hers with a kind of need that had my hands trembling as I held her tight to me. I'd never kissed *anyone*, let alone Maggie, this hard. But I felt this rampant need inside of me to claim her. I needed her to understand the true depth of her ownership over me.

And I needed her to stop fighting this. Us.

I knew she needed to be angry to face her feelings. It wasn't my favorite thing about her, but it didn't make me love her any less.

And so I gave her the time she needed and I waited.

I was always going to wait for her.

She thought she was the only one who'd hidden her feelings, but that night six years ago wasn't the first time I'd wanted her. It wasn't the second, third, or fourth either. I'd wanted her for much longer. That night was just the night I finally let myself have her because I thought it would be my only chance to taste her, to touch her the way I'd spent too many nights dreaming about. To love her the way I wanted to.

But now I'd lived a life without her and faced death head-on, and I knew that a life without her was no life at all. Now I just needed to make sure she fully understood that I was hers.

Now and every day after.

I picked her up by the back of her thighs, and she immediately wrapped her legs around me. Carefully, while still kissing her—because I refused to stop—I carried her up the stairs to her apartment.

The door was unlocked, which shouldn't have surprised me. This was Meadowbrook, and I was pretty sure nobody locked their doors here.

Our kiss was hungry and urgent, almost rough with our lips mashing against each other. Our teeth occasionally clacked as both of us fought for dominance of the kiss.

This was a battle I would fight with her for the rest of my life—happily.

I threw her on the bed. "Take off your clothes."

She didn't hesitate, and I thought my heart would swell three times its size at her willingness to strip in front of me without hesitation or protest. It also eased a tension inside me that had been there since I returned to Meadowbrook. She wasn't fighting this—me—anymore.

While she removed her clothes, I removed mine, grateful that the room was dark since it was so late and we hadn't bothered to turn any lights on.

She wasn't fighting this anymore, but that didn't

mean she was ready to see my tattoo. I knew once she did, she'd have a lot of questions, and I didn't want to answer those right now. All I wanted to do was to taste her again and feel her perfect body against mine. I wanted to slide inside her warm heat and relish in the feeling of bliss and home that only she made me feel.

Grabbing her ankle, I pulled her roughly down the bed until I could lean over her, loving the little squeak she made at the move. Her eyes were bright, and I could practically see the challenge glinting in her gaze. Before she could say anything, I sealed my lips over hers again, and once more, it was like a spark to start a wildfire.

We were all limbs and moans as we kissed and fought, her nails scraping along my back, even as her legs tightened around my hips.

I groaned and slapped her butt, half expecting her to be affronted or at least act that way. But she surprised me as a deep moan escaped her throat and she rocked her pussy against my hard cock. She was soaked already.

The air seemed to shift, our kiss growing soft and languid as I laid her back on the bed and covered her body with mine, simultaneously rocking my hips and coating my cock in her arousal.

I pulled back for a moment and she blinked up at me, her eyes clear and open and formidable.

"Fuck, Maggie," I whispered, my voice hoarse. "You fucking own me. Do you get it now?"

"I'm starting to," she whispered.

I leaned down to kiss her again, pouring all the love and longing I felt into our kiss. Her arms wrapped around my neck, pulling me closer as our tongues danced together.

My fingers shook slightly as I trailed my hand down her side, over the curve of her hip, and across her thigh. She felt like a dream that I still couldn't believe was real. She was here, in my arms, kissing me back, and finally—fucking finally—admitting that this was more.

It always had been.

"I want to ride you," she murmured against my lips.

Fuck, I wanted that too. I didn't hesitate to roll onto my back, pulling her with me, so she sat straddled over my stomach. It was too dark to see any details, but that almost added to the sensation of having her sit astride me. I could feel her, hear her, smell her arousal perfuming the air, but I couldn't see what she was about to do next, and that had my blood heating in anticipation.

Her long dark hair fell across my chest as she leaned down to kiss my sternum, then followed the light dusting of chest hair down to my belly button. My body was tense as I held myself back from begging her to sit on my cock and ride me hard until we both came. But I wanted her to do whatever she wanted, even if the slow, seductive way she kissed down my body felt like the most exquisite torture.

And then she slid those soft hands around my hard cock, and I couldn't have stopped the groan that escaped if I tried. I shuddered as her tongue licked up my stiff length, then slid my hands in her hair, desperate to touch her.

"Fuck, Mags. You don't know what you do to me."

"I have an idea." I could hear the smirk in her words.

Any other thoughts I possessed evaporated as she took me into her mouth and sucked. I gripped her hair tighter—not enough to hurt, but enough to keep me slightly grounded—and tried to say the alphabet backward, but her mouth and tongue were wreaking havoc on my mind as pleasure coursed sharp and thick up my spine.

"Fuck." She was going to make me come if she kept this up.

As if she knew how close I was to the edge, she pulled her mouth off with a pop. My body sagged back on the bed as I tried to catch my breath, even as the denied orgasm made my balls ache.

She kissed back up my body until her pussy was gliding against my cock.

"Did sucking me off make you that wet?" I asked, my voice gruff with need.

"Yes," she whispered, rocking her hips back and forth, soaking me with her arousal.

"Maggie, I'm too close, baby. If you keep doing that, I'm going to come before you."

"I don't want to stop," she said, her own voice throaty as if she was lost to the pleasure already.

I squeezed her thighs, not wanting her to stop either, but also not wanting her to do something she wasn't ready for.

"I need to grab a condom."

She didn't even hesitate as she leaned over me. "I

want to feel you bare," she whispered against my lips, and my heart nearly stalled in my chest.

I pulled back to look into her eyes. "No condom?"

She shook her head, but spoke anyway. "No condom," she whispered. "Did you mean it when you said you hadn't been with anyone since me?"

"Yes."

"I haven't been with anyone in two years, and my last checkup was all clear. I'm on birth control, so we don't have to worry about that."

"I'm not worried." I'd have a baby with her in a heartbeat. If anything, I wanted a family with her as soon as she'd let me.

She nuzzled against me, and her voice was tinged with a mix of need and vulnerability. "I don't want anything between us."

She slid her pussy against my cock until I was pushing the tip into her, and we both sucked in a sharp breath. I looked into her eyes, seeing the love and desire I felt reflected back at me. It was time I finally said the words out loud that I'd held close to my heart for far too long. Maggie deserved to hear how loved she was every day, not loved in secret. From now on, I wanted her to feel my love with every breath she breathed. I never wanted her to doubt how much she meant to me ever again.

"I love you, Maggie," I whispered. "I've always loved you."

I pushed up into her slowly, feeling her body stretch to accommodate me. She was so tight, so warm, so perfect. She sat up, placed her hands on my chest, and then sunk down on my cock until her pelvis met mine.

We both moaned as pleasure arched between us. The feel of her bare was otherworldly.

She began to move, up and down my cock before she adjusted and switched to a rocking motion that made me nearly come out of my skin. Her moans grew as she took her pleasure with my body, and I was right there with her, one hand gripping her thigh, while the other moved to her breast. I pinched her taut, pink nipple, and her hips stuttered as she cried out my name in pleasure. Her orgasm rolled through her, and I couldn't fight its pull as her pussy squeezed my cock with everything it had. I came with a roar, my body shaking as I poured myself into her.

We collapsed together, our bodies still joined, our hearts beating as one. I kissed her gently, feeling the love between us like a tangible thing.

"You're it for me, Maggie," I whispered. "You've always been it for me."

13

MAGGIE

I wasn't sure how long I'd been asleep when a shout woke me up.

"No!"

I rolled over to find Cody thrashing beside me, his eyes still closed but his face filled with distress. The sheets were caught around his legs, and his head twisted back and forth.

"Cody." I placed a hand on his arm and found him covered in sweat. I was tempted to turn the light on, but I wasn't sure if that would make it better or worse.

Indecision plagued me as he continued to thrash and shout. I couldn't sit here and watch him suffer with whatever nightmare was going on in his head.

I shook his arm and shouted his name. "Cody!"

He sat up with a jolt, his eyes wide open and his chest heaving like he'd just run a marathon.

His eyes frantically took in what little he could see in my dark room.

"Cody?" I said his name softly, not wanting to spook him.

At the sound of my voice, his shoulders sagged and he buried his head in his hands. "I'm sorry."

I scooted closer, wrapping my arms around his shoulders and hugging him tight. He held his body stiff at first before finally giving in to my embrace.

"You have nothing to apologize for."

He huffed out a humorless laugh. "I can't even go a weekend without a nightmare."

I placed a gentle kiss to his shoulder. "Want to talk about it?"

I expected him to shut me down, but instead, he turned his head and kissed me. "Only if you let me hold you while I do. I need the reminder that I'm not over there, that I didn't die, and that I wasn't too late to tell you I love you."

My heart squeezed painfully in my chest at the heartache in his voice.

We settled back against the pillows, snuggling together with his arms wrapped around me and our legs intertwined.

"I was on a mission overseas a few months ago. We'd been at a local village meeting with the elders to see what we could do to help since we were planning to set up a presence there. Talks went well, but we stayed later than we originally planned, hanging out with the local villagers and kicking a ball around with some kids. Our section commander told us we needed to wrap things up and get back to the forward operating base. We left and took the main road back to base. Things were going exactly to plan until the last truck in our convoy exploded.

"You're trained for these things, but nothing can fully prepare you for the reality when it happens. When the truck exploded, the whole convoy stopped. I got out, along with another guy from my vehicle, and we joined another soldier, Connor Jackson, from the truck that had been right in front of the explosion. We were supposed to provide security and treat the wounded until medevac showed up. Jackson when to check on Hurley—the driver of the truck that was hit—while Hinson and I made our way to him. But then out of nowhere, a shot fired, and what I thought was water flecked across my face. I ducked behind the nearest vehicle and when I turned to Hinson, I realized it wasn't water."

My gut clenched at his meaning, even as my heart ached at the pain in his voice. He was trying to tell me what happened with detachment, but the fear of that day flowed like an undercurrent with every word.

"Hinson was down. I got to Jackson as he was pulling Hurley out of the burned vehicle. Hurley's right leg was a mess from the explosion, and now the gunfire felt like it was endless. We got to a ditch with Hurley. The vehicle Jackson was in had moved back to offer us some covering fire while I tied a tourniquet to Hurley's thigh to try to stanch the bleeding. Hurley passed out, and that's when a rocket-propelled grenade hit the number two vehicle in the convoy. Two guys gone in the span of a heartbeat. Jackson left Hurley with me to try to put some fire down range, toward the hillside, then ducked for cover as they shot another RPG our way. It landed a few yards away, but my fucking ears were ringing. The sound was deafening."

His voice croaked and I held him tighter.

"I was desperate. We had gunfire and RPGs going off with our men dying all around us, and all I could think about was you."

Tears filled my eyes, and his arms tightened around me like he was afraid this was all a dream and he was still on that mission, facing his death.

"When the lead vehicle got hit, Jackson and I looked at each other, and I knew we were both thinking the same thing. That this was it. This was how we died. But I couldn't die because I'd never told you that I loved you."

"How'd you get out?" I asked, keeping my voice soft.

"Two Apaches and a Chinook. We'd called for our quick reaction force as soon as the first vehicle blew, but it felt like we were out there for hours before they finally showed up. The Apache gunships made quick work of the fighters on the hillside while the guys inside the Chinook gathered up our KIA. It wasn't until we got back to the FOB that we learned it had only been thirty minutes. The longest thirty minutes of my life. In half an hour, they killed twelve of our guys and injured one. Jackson and I were the only ones who just had minor scrapes for the most part. Although I think it's safe to say we also got some wicked PTSD, if my nightmares are anything to go by."

"I'm glad you made it out alive." It felt like a weak

thing to say, but I couldn't voice my fears that seemed so insignificant in the face of everything he'd gone through. But they were there, nonetheless. The what-ifs plagued me.

What if he hadn't gotten out?

What if he'd died?

What if I'd lived the rest of my life always wondering why I wasn't enough for him when that had never been the case?

"Hey," he said softly, his hand coming up to cup my face as his thumb ran soothing circles over my cheek. "I can feel your heart racing. What's going on in that beautiful head of yours?"

"Nothing," I murmured, hating how choked up my voice sounded even to my own ears.

"Don't do that. Don't pull that 'nothing' bullshit with me, Maggie. I know you better than that and it's never nothing. Tell me."

"No."

"Why not?"

"Because it makes me sound like a wimpy girl," I muttered, wincing at the petulance in my voice.

I didn't want to sound like a wimpy girl, and yet I sounded like one anyway.

Instead of being frustrated with me, he laughed. The sound soothed my frayed nerves and pointless worries. "God, I fucking love you." He followed his words with a kiss to my head, and I closed my eyes and breathed him in.

I love you too.

I was still too scared to say it out loud. But I couldn't deny that I felt it in my soul.

14

CODY

She was getting lost in her head, and I didn't want to lose her yet. If we were going to open up about the hardest things we'd experienced in the last six years, then there was something I wanted to know from her.

"Will you tell me what happened with your dad?"

She nuzzled against my chest and I closed my eyes, savoring the moment.

"He was working on the roof of his house trying to repair some damage from a tree branch that had fallen during a winter storm. I'd told him time and time again to hire someone, but you know how stubborn he can be."

I smiled. "Seems to be a Duke family trait."

She sat up and smacked me on my chest, but I didn't miss the way her lips tilted up in a soft smile before she settled her head back on my pec.

"Anyway, he slipped on some ice and hit his head on the way down. Fortunately, we had a good two feet of snow that helped cushion his fall to the ground or it could've been way worse. He was diagnosed with a trau-matic brain injury. At first, they weren't entirely sure what the impacts would be on his life. TBI symptoms can vary pretty dramatically. Most days, he's okay. His motor skills are a bit stilted and his walk a bit unsteady. His memory isn't always that great, especially short term. But sometimes, he has really bad days, with mood swings and forgetfulness so bad that it almost comes across like dementia."

"That's why you stayed here." It wasn't a question. I knew she'd never leave her dad in that kind of condition.

Did Matty know it was that bad or had she watered it down for him so he wouldn't give up the job and life he loved so much in Portland?

"Yeah. Matty was already off living his life and he seemed so happy on the phone or when we did video calls. I was still here and already helping take care of him and the bar, so it just made the most sense."

What hurt most of all was to hear the defeat in her voice—like her dreams weren't important.

"Do you wish you hadn't stayed?"

She was quiet for a long time- so long I wondered if she'd fallen asleep. Finally, she broke the silence. "I always wanted to settle down in Meadowbrook. I do love it here, even if small-town life can feel a little suffocating at times."

It felt like there was more she wanted to say but she was biting back her words.

"But..." I said, hoping it would encourage her to speak

her mind. I'd shown her the demons in my closet. Now I wanted to see hers.

"But I wish it wasn't so easy for everyone else to leave me here."

Her words hit me like a punch to the gut, knocking the wind out of me.

She wasn't just talking about her mom or Matty.

She was talking about me.

I'd made it appear like it was easy to leave her. She'd never understand how hard it had been. How that decision had haunted me completely for six years.

How it haunted me even now that I had her in my arms because of all the time we'd missed out on together.

"You aren't easy to leave, Maggie. Leaving you is the hardest thing I've ever done."

They were just words, but they were the truest words I'd ever spoken apart from telling her I loved her. Leaving her was harder than any mission I'd been on—including the one where I almost died. Even now, the thought of leaving her on Monday morning made my heart sink to my stomach because I didn't know if she'd accept the offer I was going to give her.

Maggie nuzzled closer, and I held her tight against me as her breath evened out and she fell asleep. She needed action. She needed to see that someone would fight for her. That I would fight for her.

So that's exactly what I intended to do.

15

MAGGIE

Sunday Morning

The smell of bacon woke me from a deep sleep. It was the best sleep I'd had in as long as I could remember, once we finally fell back asleep after our late-night talk in the dark.

I grabbed Cody's shirt that had been discarded on the chair at the end of my bed and slipped it on. I held the neck of it up to my nose and closed my eyes as I inhaled his scent. Tingles skittered along my nerve endings at the memories of last night. This whole weekend had felt like one of my wildest dreams. I was still wrapping my head around the fact that he genuinely seemed to want to make this work.

I padded out to the kitchen where he was standing at my stove wearing only his boxers. He looked insanely sexy making himself at home, and the sense of rightness that I'd felt when he told me he loved me last night warmed me to the core. I closed the distance between us and wrapped my arms around him, resting my cheek against his bare back.

One of his hands came to hold mine against his stomach while the other continued to flip the bacon in the skillet. Once he was done flipping them, he spun around, wrapping his arms around me.

"Will you come somewhere with me today?" he asked.

"Sure."

I wanted to soak up every moment I had with him. He'd told me he loved me, but he hadn't said he was staying, and I was painfully aware that today was our last day together.

I pulled back slightly when my gaze caught on something I hadn't noticed before. I blinked, realizing this was the first time I was seeing his bare torso in the light. Tattooed over his heart was a date—a date from six years ago that I couldn't have forgotten if I'd tried.

My gaze met his. "W-what is this?" My voice came out a faint whisper.

He swallowed thickly. "I got it not long after I left. I wanted a reminder of the significance."

My stare was focused on his face, but my heart was racing like a hummingbird's wings.

"The significance?" I knew why that date had been important to me—I'd given my V-card to the man I'd been in love with. But why was it significant for him?

"It was the day I knew for certain my heart would always belong to you."

I wasn't a weepy woman, but emotion was lodged in my throat. All this time, he'd missed me as much as I'd ached for him. It was clear as day, not just from the tattoo stamped on his chest, but from the look in his eyes. I leaned up to kiss him, hoping my kiss would tell him how much that simple tattoo meant to me.

After a quiet and peaceful breakfast with each other, we got dressed, got in his car, and he drove us along a back route to town, the same back route I loved to take so I could drive by my favorite house in Meadowbrook.

My heart gave a pang as his car slowed in front of the very farmhouse I'd been in love with for as long as I could remember. My disappointment that it sold was still fresh. Who knew when I'd get my chance to buy it again.

He parked the car and I turned to him. "What are we doing here?"

He rotated his body so he was facing me. "I think it's time I laid it all out for you."

"Okay," I said, nerves swirling like butterflies on crack in my stomach. I thought he'd already laid it out last night, and now I was nervous that I'd once again gotten my hopes up only to have them dashed.

"I didn't think I was good enough for you. That's why I left after our night together six years ago with just that one not nearly good enough note. I'd never really felt like

I belonged, like I was going anywhere. I wasn't very good at school. I couldn't provide the life for you that I wanted to, and I didn't think that your brother would ever be okay with it. He was the closest thing I had to a brother, and you two were the only stability I had in my life, so I wasn't willing to risk it—no matter how much I wanted to. I joined the army because I wanted to make something of myself. I wanted to prove that I was worthy."

He ducked his head like the next part he was about to say was extremely hard on him. "I told you last night about my mission that went south and how I almost died. In that moment, I begged the universe, God, any higher power, to save me, so that I could come back to you. So I could tell you that I love you. I have *always* loved you, and you are the only woman I will *ever* love."

My eyes watered, but I refused to let a single tear fall. I waited with bated breath for him to say more, even as impending doom filled my stomach. I felt the need to brace myself in case he ripped the rug out from under me.

"The reason I'm here for only the weekend is because that was the length of my approved leave. I have three months left on my contract, and then I'm out. I've already got a job coaching hockey at CFU, and I bought this house."

My jaw went slack. "You w-what?"

None of the words that just came out of his mouth were what I expected him to say.

"I bought this house for you. For us. I knew that you loved this house, and I have the money to buy it. I wanted to prove to you that I am staying. I'm here, even if I can't be here physically for three more months. I'm setting down roots here. I plan to come back here and be with you."

He grabbed my hand, his eyes pleading with mine. "I want to marry you, Maggie. I want to have a family with you. I want to build a life with you. I want to take you around the world if that's what you want. Let you see everything you never got to see because you stayed here to take care of your dad. I want to give you the life you've always wanted and deserved. I want to be your man for the rest of my life."

Nerves flitted across his face. "I know it's asking a lot, but I can't stomach the idea of not seeing you for another three months. I will, if there's no other option, but is there any way you can come back with me? And then when I'm officially out, we'll come back to Meadowbrook for good."

I swallowed thickly. I didn't really love the idea of being separated from him either, but my brain was buzzing with all the information he'd just dropped on me.

He bought a house—and not just any house, but my ultimate dream house.

He got a job at CFU.

He was coming back. Yes, he was only here for this one weekend, but he was coming back.

And he wanted me to go with him while he finished out his service.

Was there a way I could do it? I mean, I did have an employee who'd covered for me when I was sick.

And Joni had offered more than once to cover the bar so I could "finally take a freaking vacation," as she'd so eloquently put it.

Would she be willing to run it for three months? Maybe Sav would help.

Or was I insane for even considering it?

I held my breath waiting for her response. I'd laid it all out, but I wasn't going to force her to follow me. She had a life here, a business to run, and it was asking a lot of her to drop it all with less than a day's notice. Just to come live with me for three months before we could settle back here.

But that didn't make me hope any less.

Now that I'd had her again, I wasn't sure I'd survive three months without her.

"I need time to think about it," she said slowly. "It's not a no," she added quickly. "But it's just a lot. Two days ago, you weren't even an option as far as I was aware. I just wrapped my head around us being together, and now you're telling me you bought a house here. And not just any house, but my dream house. And you want me to leave Meadowbrook for three months. It's a lot."

"Yeah, I know. You're right. I'm sorry to throw this all on you."

She looked out the windshield at the farmhouse I knew she'd had her heart set on. I'd overheard her telling Sav and Joni once how much she wanted to buy it someday. I thought the timing was another sign from the universe that I was meant to be here with her. I mean, what were the odds that her dream house would go up for sale—and be in my budget—right as I was about to get out?

Now that I had her again, I knew it had been the right move to buy it. If we had to do long distance for three months before my discharge, then that's what I would do. But there was no going back for me. I would do whatever it took to be hers.

"Uh, I need to do some work at the bar. Can you take me back to my place so I can get my truck?" she asked.

"Yeah, sure," I said, driving us back to her apartment.

I watched her drive off with her brow furrowed in that cute little way she did when she was thinking hard. A knot of nerves tightened in my gut, but I pushed it down and drove back to Beverly's and the little cottage I'd rented for the weekend. Regardless of what Maggie chose to do, I had to pack for my flight back to base tomorrow morning. Except, when I got back to the cottage and looked around, I realized I hadn't unpacked that much to begin with, which meant I was packed and mostly ready to go in less than five minutes.

I sat heavily on the bed and pulled out my phone. I

needed something to distract me from driving to the bar to soak up every second with Maggie that I could, especially if she told me she couldn't come back to Georgia with me.

I twirled the phone between my fingers and then pulled up the number of someone I hadn't talked to in a few weeks.

In fact, we hadn't talked much at all since we'd been back from that failed mission. He was one of the few people who understood what I'd gone through and how it had knocked my world off its axis. His contract was up this week and when I'd asked him about his plans, he'd just shrugged and mentioned going back to California where he grew up. We hadn't talked much past that.

It rang a handful of times before Connor Jackson answered. "Maxwell," he said, keeping it short.

"Jackson," I responded. "How's it going, man?"

"Oh, you know, just doing my thing," he said.

"You see that therapist the CO recommended?"

He let out a chuckle that carried no humor in it. "Yeah, but only the mandatory sessions until she cleared me. I'm fine."

I doubted that was true. I didn't think either of us had been fine since our mission overseas. A glance at the rumpled bed sheets reminded me of the last time I'd slept here with Maggie in my arms. I was closer to fine than I'd been before I came back to Meadowbrook. But where that day had given me purpose and direction for where I wanted my life to go, it had seemed to do the opposite for

Connor. I was worried about him. I knew Hurley worried about him too.

"Have you talked to anybody about what happened?"

Silence filled the line.

I wasn't surprised. The therapy sessions had been mandatory just to make sure we were stable enough to still work, but we weren't required or even encouraged to talk about what happened that day. The therapist only cared about the aftermath.

Finally, as if reluctant to speak at all or acknowledge what had happened to us, he grunted out a no.

"You should consider doing it," I told him.

"Did you tell someone?" he asked.

"Yeah." I wasn't going to get into it with him. He wasn't ready—I could hear it in his voice. But I did have one final thing to say. "Don't make it be for nothing, Connor." We rarely used each other's first names, so I hoped he'd understand what I was trying to convey. "We survived. We deserve to live the lives we were meant to have."

"Yeah, Hurley told me the same thing."

It was good to hear that he was going to visit Hurley. Connor seemed to be the one who was struggling the most, despite the fact Hurley had permanent injuries, including the loss of a limb, from what happened. But sometimes it was the emotional and mental wounds we carried that weighed us down the most.

"Hey, look, I gotta go," he said.

I shouldn't have been surprised that he wanted to get off the phone so quickly. Jackson hadn't been a big talker before, but now he seemed even more closed off. I wondered what it would take for him to open up. And who would finally get through that thick wall he'd built.

Since I figured Maggie would take most of the day to sort herself out, I decided to call my real estate agent and see if I could get into the house, take a look around, and start making some plans for how to make it ours. Sitting here for the rest of the day would make me slowly go insane, especially without knowing if I'd be leaving tomorrow with my woman by my side. And after talking to Jackson, all I wanted was to feel like I was finally moving forward with my life the way it always should've been.

17

MAGGIE

Instead of going to the bar, I went to Sav's house.

Savannah Richards and I had been best friends since kindergarten, and I was pretty sure she'd been in love with Wesley—or Wes as we all called him—for just as long. They'd been together since junior high and got married right out of college, so I didn't usually come to her when I needed relationship advice because she'd only ever been with Wes. As far as Sav was concerned, love was easy and uncomplicated, which couldn't be further from my own experience. Joni was usually my go-to, but seeing as how Joni was visiting her grandma in Bozeman, I couldn't talk to her in person, and this was definitely an in-person kind of freak-out.

Sav answered her door with the usual warm and welcoming smile I'd come to always expect from her. "Maggie. Hey, did I know you were coming over?"

"Nope," I said.

Her eyes went wide as she must have seen the utter

panic on my face. "Oh boy. Come on in," she said, stepping back and letting me walk past her into her living room. I sat down on her couch while she went to the kitchen and grabbed us some waters. She set them down on the coffee table as she sat next to me. "All right, spill it. What's going on?"

"Cody Maxwell came back and told me he's in love with me and he's been in love with me the whole time and he didn't think he was good enough and that's why he left and now he bought the Smithson farmhouse and he wants us to live there and to get married but he still has three months left before he gets discharged so he just asked me to go back with him and I don't even know where back is because I didn't think to ask because I was panicking and now I'm extra panicking because I should know where he even wants me to move to because maybe that's a deal-breaker and—"

She held up a hand to stop my verbal diarrhea. "Okay, I'm gonna need you to rewind and take it one piece at a time."

So I took a deep breath and laid it all out for her. I told her about how I'd been in love with him, our night together six years ago, and everything that had happened over the course of the past two days. Had it really only been two days?

"It's crazy that I'm even considering this, isn't it?" I asked her.

She hummed.

"What does that hum mean?" I asked.

She shook her head, her lips pulling up in a soft, exasperated smile. "Relax. That hum doesn't have any double meanings. It was just a hum, Maggie."

I scrubbed my hand over my face. "Sorry. I'm freaking out here."

She chuckled. "You don't say."

"I'm sorry," I said again, more sincerely because I realized I was totally dumping on her. "I'm just..."

"You're just in love," she said. "And love has a tendency to be kind of scary."

That caught my attention because in all the time I'd known Sav, never once had she implied that love was scary. As far as I knew, love in Savannah Richards's mind was sure and constant. She'd always known that Wes was the one for her, and that seemed like a done deal. As far as I knew, they'd never even had a big fight.

Was there trouble in paradise? If Sav and Wes couldn't make it, then what hope was there for the rest of us? They were the definition of a perfect couple.

As if she could see the questions swirling in my mind, she raised a hand. "Today's not about me."

But that statement only made me want to know more. Had I missed something critical?

"Okay," she said, focusing back on my problems. "So now that you've explained everything that's going on, let's talk it out."

I gave her a look that said we'd talk about whatever was going on with her later and then took a breath. Talking it out seemed like a good idea. Hell, it was the whole reason I'd come here.

"So what do you want to do?" she asked. "Deep

down in your soul, what is it telling you to do—and not because you're afraid, or because you think you need to or should do one thing or another. What do you *want* to do?"

I knew my answer instantly, but I kept my mouth shut.

Sav placed a gentle hand on mine. "Maggie, I love you to pieces, but everything you've done has been for other people. I know you love the bar, but you took it over for your dad. Don't try to deny it," she said when I opened my mouth to protest. "You stayed in Meadowbrook because your dad needed you to take over the bar and not because you wanted to stay here. Maybe you would have ended up here eventually, but you talked endlessly about your plans after high school and college of traveling and seeing the world. Yet, you never did any of it because the bar and taking care of your dad has taken over your life. So, I'm going to ask again. What do *you* want?"

"Him," I whispered, my voice hoarse with emotions I was trying to tamp down. "I want him and I want the life in the farmhouse that he talked about this morning. I want to wake up to him making me bacon shirtless and then go out with our friends. I want to forget the hurt I felt, or better yet, I don't want that hurt to hold me back from experiencing something that could be everything I ever wanted."

"Then that's what you do," she said, her gaze soft. She made it sound so simple, but it couldn't be that easy.

Could it?

"You take what you want—what you deserve. Maggie, you deserve to be happy more than anyone I know."

"You don't think this is crazy? I mean, come on, it's me. I've never been the girl who gets what she wants, and I don't know if I can wrap my head around it."

"Just because you haven't up until now doesn't mean you don't deserve to get what you want, and it doesn't mean that you can't take what you want now. If he's here and he's offering you everything you dreamed of, then take it with both hands."

"But what about my dad and the bar?" I asked.

She shrugged, seemingly not worried at all. "What about the bar? Joni and I will take care of it. We've managed it before when you had to help with your dad's health stuff. We've got it. And we'll check on your dad and take him to any appointments if he needs it. We'll keep things going here until you get back."

"You're sure? It feels like I'm asking too much."

She shook her head. "Maggie, you never ask for *anything*. Let us take this off your plate and for once, take the leap. Fight for what you want. Go spread your wings and see somewhere else. Get out of Montana and follow the love of your life."

This was insane.

But I was going to do it anyway because she was right. I deserved my chance at a happy ending, and there had only ever been one man I wanted that ending with.

18

CODY

It was taking everything in me not to hop in my rental car and drive over to Maggie's house and bang on her door. I'd promised to give her space today to think, and I'd thought all she would need was a few hours to clear her head.

I did not expect to be staring at the clock at nine o'clock at night without a word from her.

My bag was packed by the door, and I knew I needed to head to bed soon if I was going to wake up in time to catch my flight out of Missoula, but it didn't feel right to leave Montana without her. And it sure as hell didn't feel right to even consider leaving Montana without some kind of answer from her about what our future held.

If she wasn't ready, I would wait, but I needed her to understand that in three months, I was coming back for her. I was going to live in that house and I was going to fix it up the way she'd always talked about. I would woo the shit out of her if that's what she needed because I wasn't done with Maggie Duke, not by a long shot, and I had plans that someday she'd be Maggie Maxwell.

I had just popped open a beer when a knock sounded on the door, and I rushed to open it to find Maggie standing there, a large and very full duffel bag clutched in her hands.

"Please don't break my heart again," she whispered, her eyes wide.

I was already shaking my head. "Never again," I said as I stepped into her space, grabbed her cheeks, and kissed her with all the love, all the longing, all the unspoken promises I'd kept locked away for so long. Her lips were soft and warm, yielding to mine as she let out a soft sigh. The taste of her, sweet and familiar, sent a rush of desire coursing through my veins.

I kicked the door shut behind her and backed her up against it, never breaking our kiss. The duffel bag dropped to the floor with a thud as her hands found their way to my hair, tugging gently in a way that had desire zipping down my spine. I pressed my body against hers, feeling her soft curves mold to me, and I knew I was home. This was where I belonged, where I'd always belonged.

She was my reason for living—for surviving the desert—and I would never let her go.

"Cody," she whispered against my lips, and the vulnerability in her voice made me pause. I looked into her beautiful eyes that had always held me captive. "You were my first, and I want you to be my last."

"Your first?"

She nodded.

My heart jumped to my throat as guilt ate away at my stomach lining. "You were a virgin that night? At the cabin?"

She nodded again.

"You never said anything." My voice broke as I spoke and realized how thoroughly I'd ruined that moment for her. She'd given me the most amazing gift, and I'd let her down in the worst way possible afterward. I dropped my forehead to hers and cupped her cheeks. "I'm so sorry, Maggie. I didn't know. I—"

She cut me off with a kiss. "I know. Let's not look back anymore. I just want to move forward and think about our future. I think we've let the past hurt us enough, don't you?"

Now it was my turn to nod.

I would never understand what I'd done to deserve this woman, but I would spend the rest of my life being the man she deserved. I would go to the ends of the earth to make her happy because I never wanted her to doubt my love ever again.

My hands trailed down her cheeks, her neck, her shoulders, until they found the hem of her shirt. I pulled back just enough to lift it over her head, revealing her smooth, creamy skin. I dipped my head, trailing kisses down her neck, her collarbone, her sternum, until I reached the swell of her perfect breasts. I cupped one in my hand, kneading gently as I took the other into my mouth, sucking and licking until her nipple hardened into a tight peak.

Maggie arched beneath me, a soft moan escaping her lips. Her fingers tangled in my hair, holding me close as I lavished attention on her breasts, switching from one to the other until she was writhing beneath me. I could feel her heart racing, her breath coming in quick pants. Fuck, she was close already, but I wasn't ready to let her go over the edge just yet.

I dropped to my knees in front of her, my hands tracing the curves of her hips, her thighs, before finding the button of her jeans. I looked up at her, our eyes locking as I undid her pants and then slid the zipper down. She bit her lip, her chest heaving with anticipation. I tugged her jeans down, revealing her long, lean legs, and I couldn't resist running my hands over her smooth skin.

I leaned in, inhaling deeply as I pressed a soft kiss to the lace fabric of her panties. She gasped, her hips bucking against my mouth. I hooked my fingers into the waistband and pulled them down, revealing her completely to me. I sat back on my heels, taking a moment to appreciate the sight of her, naked and vulnerable, her chest rising and falling rapidly, her eyes dark with desire. I would never tire of this. I craved the taste of her constantly, especially after so long without.

"You're so beautiful, Maggie," I murmured, my voice husky with emotion. "I've dreamed of this moment, of you, every night since I left. I never stopped loving you, never stopped wanting you."

Her eyes were filled with vulnerability, but the fear and insecurity I'd seen there before were gone. "I love you, Cody. I always have. I always will."

My heart wanted to beat out of my chest as a euphoria I didn't know was possible surged through me. I still wasn't sure I deserved her love, but I was going to take it anyway.

I stood up, scooping her into my arms, and carried her to the bed, laying her down gently before stripping out of my own clothes. I needed to feel her skin against mine, needed to be as close to her as possible.

I crawled onto the bed, settling between her legs, my body covering hers. I braced myself on my elbows, looking down into her eyes, seeing my own love and desire reflected back at me. Her lips were too tempting to ignore, so I leaned down, capturing them in a slow, deep kiss. She wrapped her arms around me, her nails lightly scratching my back.

I broke away from her lips, trailing kisses down her neck, her collarbone, her chest, until I reached her breasts again. They were quickly becoming one of my favorite parts of her. I'd never gotten to explore her during our first night together—not like I'd gotten to this weekend. And I couldn't wait to spend a lifetime learning every inch of her body.

I took one nipple into my mouth, swirling my tongue around it, feeling it harden beneath my touch. Maggie arched beneath me, a soft moan escaping her lips and her breath coming in quick pants.

I continued my journey down her body, kissing every

inch of her skin as if it were sacred ground. When I reached her hips, I looked up at her, our eyes locking as I settled between her legs. I ran my hands up her thighs, feeling her tremble beneath my touch. I leaned in, inhaling deeply, her scent filling my senses, before running my tongue along her slit.

She gasped, her hips bucking against my mouth. I explored her folds with my tongue, licking and sucking until I found her clit. Her moans grew louder, her body tensing as her muscles clenched around my fingers. I sucked her needy little bud into my mouth, flicking it with my tongue as I pumped my fingers faster. She cried out, her body convulsing as waves of pleasure washed over her. I continued to lick and suck gently, riding out her orgasm with her until she collapsed back onto the bed, her body sated and limp.

I kissed my way back up her body as her breathing returned to normal. When I reached her lips, I kissed her deeply, letting her taste herself on my tongue. She moaned softly, her arms wrapping around me as she pulled me close.

I settled between her legs, the head of my cock poised at her entrance before I canted my hips and slid into her slowly, feeling her body stretch to accommodate me. Her wet heat was deliciously tight and so perfect, I had to fight against the urge to come. I buried myself to the hilt, our bodies joined completely, and we both gasped, our breaths mingling as we held each other tightly.

I began to move, sliding in and out of her slowly, our

bodies rocking together in perfect rhythm. Her legs wrapped around my hips and she dug her heels into my ass, urging me deeper. I complied, picking up the pace as our bodies moved together.

"Fuck, Mags, you feel too good, baby. You take my cock so well."

Her pussy fluttered around my cock as another orgasm grew closer. I was close too, the pressure building at the base of my spine and my balls drawing up tight. I reached between us, finding her clit with my thumb and circling it gently because I needed her to come with savage desperation.

With a few swirls over her clit, her body convulsed, her muscles clenching around me as she came again, crying out my name. The sound of her pleasure sent me over the edge, and I came with a roar, my body shaking as I poured myself into her.

I rolled onto my side, pulling her with me so that we were face to face, and kissed her gently. A bone-deep sense of contentment settled inside me.

I was finally home.

The next morning I drove to the airport with Maggie's hand in mine the whole way there. As we walked to our gate, I held her close to me.

Since she'd showed up at the cottage door, everything had felt right. We were going on an adventure, and we were going to be on it together, like we always should have been. I had finally gotten it right and had my woman by my side where she'd always belonged. My home wasn't a place; it was a person.

It was Maggie.

And I couldn't wait to see what our future held.

EPILOGUE
MAGGIE

Five Years Later

"Come on, Lumberjack Alumni!" I screamed.

It was just supposed to be a fun reunion game, but I was still competitive and wanted the alumni to win. Mainly so my husband would lose the bet we made before we came to the game tonight. Cody claimed his current players could outperform his past players, but I had a soft spot for the boys who'd been on his original team, and I wanted to see them win, especially with their wives and kids in tow.

I'd never come to these reunion weekends until Cody and I got together since I never went to college and Cody had dropped out of CFU before he could graduate, so he wasn't technically an alumni. But since he'd become the coach and helped lead the CFU hockey team to multiple victories, it had become part of his job to participate in these homecoming reunion weekend games.

This also happened to be the first weekend where his original team of players had all come back.

Joni and Sav sat on either side of me while I held my daughter, Olivia, on my lap. She was two and had been a surprise, but she was the best surprise I'd ever gotten.

Becoming a mother had been an experience, to say the least. The lack of sleep was a mind fuck, but more than that I loved my daughter with so much of myself that it made it harder to rationalize how my own mother could have left me the way she did. I didn't know how many nights I stayed up holding Livy, staring down at her precious little face, thinking there had to be something fundamentally wrong with my mother that she couldn't find that connection with her children the way I had found it so easily with mine.

Cody was already talking about trying for another, but one was a challenge enough, especially with running the bar, which had now become a bar and restaurant.

I had no idea that when Cody returned to town, he would make every single dream I'd ever carried in my heart come true. No one was a bigger cheerleader for my dreams than my husband.

It started when he gave me the farmhouse and we worked together to fix it up and make it our own. After that, he helped me raise the funds to make the repairs and upgrades I wanted to the bar and truly—finally—made it what I'd always wanted it to be.

It would always remain Duke's in honor of my father, but now it was Duke's Bar & Grill, and I hoped to someday leave it as a legacy if one of my children wanted it.

Livy clapped excitedly, bringing my attention back to the game.

It was fun to see the players—both current and past—start to really get into it on the ice. I was sure the taunts from the crowd that had gathered helped encourage the competition. The current team wanted to prove what they believed to be true—that they were the best hockey team CFU had ever had—while the former players wanted to prove they still had it.

Foster Kane, the former captain, was a force to be reckoned with. He was a bit bulkier than he used to be, but he still had the speed and agility that had made him a star player during his time at CFU. Cody always told me Foster was the reason he didn't quit after his first year as coach—when Foster set his mind to something, he didn't give up, and it had pushed Cody not to give up either.

Foster intercepted a pass from one of the current players, spinning around and skating toward the goal with a burst of speed that caught the opposing team—and most of the crowd if the sudden gasps were any indication—off guard.

Foster closed in on the goalie, a young freshman—Brewster—who looked like he was trying his best not to be intimidated. Foster faked a shot that the young goalie fell for, and Foster slipped the puck into the net with a smooth, practiced move. I winced. I'm sure Cody would run a ton of drills at their next practice to make sure that didn't happen in a real game. The alumni section of the crowd went wild, chanting Foster's name as he skated back to the center ice, a wide grin on his face.

The current team quickly rallied, their pride stung. They began to play with renewed vigor, their passes faster, their shots more aggressive. The alumni, however, were not about to let the "youngsters" show them up. They matched the current team's intensity, their own passes and shots just as fierce.

What had started out as a friendly match became an absolute nail-biter with most of the crowd up on their feet cheering on the players.

In the final seconds of the game, Foster made one last push toward the goal. He was met by the current team's captain, a senior named Dillon, who was known for his fierce competitive streak. The two players faced off, their eyes locked in a battle of wills. And then Foster grinned, his eyes crinkling underneath his mask, and Dillon took control of the puck, driving it toward the alumni side of the ice and besting Harrison "Gordy" Gordon, the goalie for the alumni.

The arena erupted in cheers from current CFU students as they celebrated their victory. Foster skated over to the side where his wife was standing with their four-month-old baby. The matching smiles that filled their faces told me all I needed to know about how well they were doing as a couple.

Cody walked over to where I was sitting instead of the benches where he'd been during the game. "Looks like I won that bet."

I laughed, shaking my head in mock exasperation. "I suppose you did."

He grinned, leaning in to press a quick kiss to my lips, then moved his mouth to my ear and murmured, "After Livy goes down for bed tonight, prepare to pay up with that sweet pussy of yours. I plan to feast like a starving man."

My lips parted in a silent gasp as my heart fluttered and my core throbbed for the pleasure I knew he could deliver.

"Don't threaten me with a good time," I choked out, finally finding my voice.

He tilted his head back, letting out a deep, throaty laugh that made my chest feel light. Then he scooped up our giggling daughter, and I melted even more. There was nothing sexier than watching Cody be an incredible father.

Players came over—past and present—to talk to him, and all the while he held Livy in his arms. Cody's first love was always going to be me and our daughter, but I knew hockey and this team had become an integral part of him. The pay was shit, and I wasn't a huge fan of the commute in the winter, but he was happy and thriving here. The university athletic director had even been looking for other ways to get him involved on campus so they could give him a pay bump. He was now working with veterans as they returned to school so they could find careers post-military life.

Cody's gaze slid to mine as he gestured to me. "You

guys remember my wife, Maggie," he said with pride in every inch of his voice.

I'd always thought I'd been confident before, but there was something about having your partner be proud of you that helped you stand just a little bit taller. I carried myself with more confidence knowing I wasn't the only one who believed in me and my dreams. Someone else believed in me too. Sometimes he believed in me more than I did.

"Baby, you remember Foster?" he asked before naming off some of the other alumni players I was familiar with. As if I could forget that year.

It had only been a few years since I'd last seen them and yet somehow these boys had all grown up. They no longer had any semblance of boyish features. They were men now with their women at their sides, building their lives, and I was proud of how far they'd come.

Cody slapped Foster on the back. "We'll get together for a team dinner before you guys all do your own thing, okay?"

"Sure thing, Coach," Foster said.

Cody shook hands with his players both current and past and then guided me out of the rink. Our daughter fell asleep in the back seat on the drive home while Cody yammered on and on about what he'd heard from the guys, the shit-talking on the ice, and how happy he was.

He grabbed my hand and brought it to his mouth, kissing the back, his eyes still on the road. "Thank you," he said. I furrowed my brow, but before I could speak, he elaborated. "Thank you for taking a leap of faith with me, for loving me and building this incredible life with me. I could never have done any of this without you by my side."

I smiled. "I'd just been thinking the same thing earlier."

"You mean that you couldn't do the bar without me?" he asked.

"No, that you couldn't do any of this without me."

He chuckled. In fact, we both laughed because we both knew that our mutual success was definitely because of our support of each other. We were stronger as a couple than we'd ever been on our own. We held each other close and lifted each other up when times were hard. My dad's health had continued to decline, and I wasn't sure anything could quite strain a marriage like having a sick parent to take care of. But even when I got short and snippy with him, Cody was there, and he knew that it wasn't because I didn't love him or was truly mad at him. He understood that it was because I was scared and because becoming the parent for your parent and watching them decline was hard, especially when they were the only one you had left.

When we got home, Cody grabbed our daughter from her car seat, and I put my hand to my chest as I watched him carry her sleeping form inside, curled in his arms.

He was the most doting father I could have ever asked to have for my child, and while I wasn't exactly ready right this second to have another one, I knew without a doubt I did want more because he would be an amazing father to all of our kids.

I had no doubt about that.

Once Olivia was put to bed and we'd done our nighttime routine, we curled up in our own big bed in the beautiful farmhouse that we were constantly working on. It had come a long way in the last five years, but the thing about old houses was that they always had something else that needed fixing.

Then Cody followed through on exactly what he promised from winning the bet earlier, just as he'd kept every single promise he'd ever made since that one weekend five years ago.

BONUS EPILOGUE

Maggie

I should have known better than to trust that winter was finally over when Cody recommended we do a weekend getaway at my family's cabin—the very same cabin where I'd given Cody my virginity eight years ago.

The weather in Montana had finally turned around and even though there was still some snow dotting the mountain landscape that surrounded our small town, I was certain the worst of the snow was behind us. It was April, after all.

But nope.

Heaven forbid mountain weather be predictable.

We'd had weeks with over fifty degrees and sunny weather, so of course the day we arrived at the cabin, the weather took a turn. The temp dropped thirty degrees and it had been snowing non-stop for the last five hours.

The wind howled outside, rattling the windows.

Thick flakes pelted against the glass, and I could barely see past the front porch.

"Happy spring, my ass," I muttered as I peered out into the white abyss. That was the last time I listened to the local weather forecaster.

Cody stretched out on the worn leather couch, his arms crossed behind his head like he didn't have a single care in the world. He was always so damn comfortable, no matter the situation. A blizzard could be raging outside, but if he had a fire, a beer, and me in the same general vicinity, he acted like life couldn't get any better.

I envied that about him. My mind felt like it was constantly keeping track of things for the bar and home repairs. I knew he thought about it too, but it seemed like he had the ability to quiet his mind when he wanted, which seemed so unfair.

"Glaring out the window won't make the snow stop." His voice was thick with amusement.

I turned, leveling him with that same glare. "We're stuck here, Cody. Stuck. What if this lasts for days? We have no reception out here and what if James or Ben need help with the bar and they can't reach me?"

He stood up and walked over to me. "They wouldn't have been able to reach you anyway because, as you said, we don't have reception out here. And they're both competent at their jobs. They can handle the bar. Weren't they the ones who told you that you needed a break?"

"Yes," I grumbled.

"And here we are, taking a break." he said, grinning.

He ducked his head, his lips brushing against my earlobe. "Maybe the snow is conspiring with James and Ben to keep you from cutting your vacation short."

He kissed behind my ear and I felt myself melting against him. Maybe it wasn't so bad being trapped in the cabin. At least we were together. The cabin was fully stocked for the weekend, so we wouldn't need anything, and knowing mountain weather, the snow wouldn't last more than a day or two before it let up.

Hell, tomorrow we could wake up to it being in the fifties again.

I spun in Cody's arms and melted even more at the heated gleam in his gray eyes.

He looked ridiculously hot with his scruffy beard and his long-sleeved shirt that sported the CFU hockey logo and fit his biceps like a dream.

Without a word, he grabbed my hand and walked backward until he was sitting back on the couch. His heated gaze didn't leave mine as he tugged me down onto his lap and wrapped his arms around me.

The warmth of his body seeped into mine, and despite my lingering frustration, I relaxed against him.

"See? That's better," he murmured against my hair. "Now I get you all to myself completely uninterrupted for at least two days."

I swallowed hard. The way he was looking at me... it was dangerous. That slow, knowing smirk. That heat in his eyes. I knew exactly where this was heading.

The air between us shifted, crackling like the fire in the hearth.

Outside, the wind howled. But inside, Cody's hands were warm, his touch familiar. He pulled me closer and when his lips brushed against mine, my breath caught.

Cody's kiss deepened, his tongue exploring my mouth with a hunger that made arousal pool between my legs. I responded in kind, my hands sliding up his chest, feeling the hard muscles beneath his shirt. His fingers tangled in my hair, pulling me closer, and I could feel his desire pressing against me.

Breaking the kiss, I looked into his eyes, seeing the raw need reflected in them. I smiled, a slow, teasing grin, and began to unbutton his shirt. His breathing hitched as I leaned down to kiss his chest, my tongue flicking against his skin. He tasted salty and warm, and I wanted more.

Cody's hands moved to my hips, guiding me as I rocked over his covered erection. He let out a deep groan as his hands slipped under my sweater and he pushed it up and over my head. The firelight cast a warm glow on my skin, and Cody's eyes drank me in like I was the most beautiful thing he'd ever seen.

Despite our rocky start, no man had ever made me feel as cherished as Cody did.

I reached behind me, unclasping my bra and letting it fall to the floor. Cody's hands cupped my breasts, his thumbs brushing against my nipples and sending jolts of pleasure through me. I arched my back, pressing into his touch, and he took advantage, capturing one nipple in his mouth, sucking and teasing until I was panting.

His hands moved to my jeans, unbuttoning them and helping me slide them off. I got off his lap to kick them aside, leaving me in nothing but a thin scrap of lace that left little to the imagination. Cody's eyes darkened as he took me in. His hungry gaze met mine at the same time that he hooked his fingers in the waistband and pulled the panties down my legs.

I stood before him completely naked, and instead of feeling vulnerable, I felt beautiful and desired.

He quickly shucked his own pants until he was sitting on the couch just as naked as I was.

"Come here," he said, his voice ragged.

Without hesitation, I straddled his lap and ground my wet pussy against his hard cock. His hands gripped my hips, urging me on, as I held the sides of his neck and kissed him with all the passion only he brought out in me.

Pulling back slightly, I wrapped my hand around his cock, stroking slowly, teasingly. He groaned as his head fell back against the couch.

"Maggie," he whispered, his voice hoarse with need.

I positioned myself over him, rubbing the head of his cock over my clit and making us both shiver from the tease of pleasure. Slowly, I slid down, taking him in inch by inch. Cody's hands gripped my hips tighter, his eyes locked on mine.

"'That's it, baby. Fuck, you take my cock so good," his words were a rough growl, as his pupils seemed to dilate.

I began to move, riding him slowly at first, then faster as the pleasure built, and I lost myself to the sensation of being so intimately connected with him.

The cabin filled with the sounds of our lovemaking, the crackling fire, and the howling wind outside. Cody's hands were everywhere, touching, caressing, driving me wild. His lips followed, kissing my chest and breasts before taking the tight bud of my nipple into his mouth. I leaned back, changing the angle, and he hit a spot deep inside me that made me gasp.

"Right there," I panted, and Cody obliged, thrusting up to meet me, hitting that spot over and over again. "Oh fuck."

I was so close.

The pleasure built, coiling tighter and tighter until it exploded, washing over me in waves. I cried out, my body shaking as I came. Cody followed soon after, his body tensing as he found his own release.

I collapsed against him, our bodies slick with sweat, and our hearts pounding in sync. Cody's arms wrapped around me, and he held me close as we caught our breath. The storm outside raged on, but in here, everything was perfect.

He pulled the soft fleece blanket that was draped over the back of the couch over our bodies and shifted us so we were cuddling horizontally on the couch. With Cody's strong arms wrapped around me and his front to my back, I watched the fire flicker and let the warm sensation of being loved fill me.

Cody traced slow, lazy circles on my bare shoulder, his voice thick with satisfaction. "You still mad we're snowed in?"

I rotated around so we were chest to chest and met his gaze. "Mmm. I think I might need another orgasm before I decide."

He grinned, his fingers brushing a stray piece of hair from my face. "I think I can make that happen."

I sighed, nuzzling against his chest, letting the warmth of him and the fire lull me into something close to sleep.

Maybe this vacation hadn't been a terrible idea after all.

Breaking the Rules Series

Only a Kiss

Just for Tonight

About Last Night

ABOUT THE AUTHOR

Cadence Keys is a bestselling steamy romance author. When she's not coming up with plots for her books, she's chasing her rambunctious toddlers around or cuddling with her husband. She loves writing heartfelt stories with relatable characters and a guaranteed happily ever after.

Learn more about her and her books on her website: www.cadencekeys.com

- facebook.com/cadencekeysauthor
- x.com/cadencewrites
- instagram.com/cadencekeysauthor
- bookbub.com/profile/cadence-keys
- goodreads.com/cadencekeysauthor
- patreon.com/CadenceKeys

Made in the USA
Coppell, TX
03 April 2025

47867444R00073